D0201693

SEVEN LIVES
AND ONE GREAT
LOVE

Lena Divani

SEVEN LIVES AND ONE GREAT LOVE:
MEMOIRS OF A CAT

*Translated from the Modern Greek
by Konstantine Matsoukas*

Europa
editions

Europa Editions
214 West 29th Street
New York, N.Y. 10001
www.europaeditions.com
info@europaeditions.com

Copyright @ 2013 by Lena Divani – Kastaniotis Editions S.A., Athens
First Publication 2014 by Europa Editions

Translation by Konstantine Matsoukas
Original title: Εγώ, ο Ζάχος Ζάχαρης
Translation copyright © 2014 by Europa Editions

Library of Congress Cataloging in Publication Data is available
ISBN 978-1-60945-197-4

Divani, Lena
Seven Lives and One Great Love

Book design and cover illustration by Emanuele Ragnisco
www.mekkanografici.com
Cover illustration from photo by Sergei Didok © Sergei Didok/iStock
Page illustrations by Alekos Papadatos © Alekos Papadatos

Prepress by Grafica Punto Print – Rome

Printed in the USA

CONTENTS

To those who are at this moment
squeezing oranges for someone they love.

If I die before you
which is all but certain
then in the moment
before you will see me
become someone dead
in a transformation
as quick as a shooting star's
I will cross over into you
and ask you to carry
not only your own memories
but mine too until you
too lie down and erase us
both together into oblivion.

GALWAY KINNELL, *Promissory Note*

MOMMY DEAREST

Though I run the risk of seeming disrespectful and ungrateful, I might as well confess it: I started planning my escape from the family home the moment I laid eyes on my progenitor. That lady (for want of a better word) was an alley cat, ugly as can be, thin and sickly, with one good eye and molting fur the color of nondescript rubbish. Darwin's shame. A bottomless pit of aggression and fear. Cat lovers would woo her to try and feed her and she would launch into an attack. A bellicose ingrate and rude to boot. What business did I have with that? The only smart choices she ever made were: a) to have sex with my father; and, b) to hunker down in a nook of the enormous garden of the corpulent, cat-loving Mrs. Sweetie, to give birth to us.

My father, whom unfortunately I never met but fortunately had sex appeal in spades, must have been of noble extraction, a pure-blooded Turk from Ankara, with a pedigree. I am nevertheless prepared to bet he was all white, with a gleam in his eye, and a handsome devil. What attracted him to that lowlife tramp, my mother, only the Lord knows. In all likelihood, he was a bourgeois de salon who slipped out of his mansion one day, to see if he would make the grade out in the streets, had a run-in with the hood and realized how unforgiving street law can be. There he was, my hapless progenitor, wallowing in self-pity, when mother turned up and restored his self-esteem. Naturally, he was taken in by her street wise savvy, what momma's boy wouldn't be? Because, the truth be told, though mom may have been an eyesore, her street smarts were beyond reproach. She happened to be in heat and she deigned to allow him admission to the club of her many lovers, so she could add a blue blood to the random pool of genes she copped. The outcome was me myself, as white as vanilla ice-cream, a noble bastard, the four-legged exception in a mob of crooked, malformed and hideous siblings who stared at me mistrustfully. And smart to boot. Indeed, a genius.

WHAT A GENIUS DOES TO PROTECT HIS WITS

It's simple really: one chooses one's parents. Freud's extrapolations may not have wide currency in our world, but our instincts are more acute than yours. I was a blind newborn behind Mrs. Sweetie's bushes, and I already knew that the life of tramping and cat fights would be pure hell and that my purpose in life was in danger of being compromised. As soon as I opened my eyes I knew for sure that my siblings might as well be called Cruddy, Scum and Misery. I, on the other hand, was the living vindication of Mendel's law. And it never did anyone any good, being that much different from the rest. Would an Eskimo seek happiness in Ethiopia? Urgent conclusion: I needed to beat it ASAP.

But where to? That was the question. I knew that one's environment is not merely important, it is all-decisive: if you spend your time frolicking in the lake, sooner or later you turn into a fish. Which is to say, I wasn't choosing a home, I was choosing a life. Take William Burroughs' cat as a case in point. There's no need to wonder why she chose to live with him. Yes, he was mildly deranged. Yes, he shot at his wife in jest. But his cat, he treated like the queen of Sheba. Rumor has it that he was even more fond of her ladyship than he was of snorting Benzedrine. Most importantly, he made a place for her in feline history. I bet you have all seen the pictures of her ladyship atop the mythical junkie's typewriter. So, then, well done, Miss Burroughspuss. You were right on target.

Sylvia Plath's cat, on the other hand, just plain blew it. She weighed up her mistress as a gentle soul and a huge talent, and thought to adopt her. Overjoyed to have hit on such a gem, she overlooked one basic element—the poet was at odds with her very skin. She had been hell bent on doing herself in since the age of twenty. She tried it once, twice, well, eventually she managed it. She ended up with her head in the oven and the cat ended up wailing alongside two babies, desperate and an orphan. Thanks, but no thanks: I myself, I could do without such drama.

At this point, there is one thing I need to come clean about: the popular rumor is true. We don't make a big deal of it but we do, actually, have seven lives. If you've met one of those breathtakingly stupid cats that break their neck falling from the eighth story while chasing pigeons, then you know what we're like during our first, and in some cases our second, life. Between you and me, I personally was such a nitwit in my first life that I kept attacking not a real bird (an annoying canary called Babe) but its shadow! I broke my nails against the wall daily. Imbecile! It embarrasses me to even think about it. Thankfully, we come out wiser in each life and by the seventh, we really do honor to our place in the food chain. We are no longer pupils but, rather, we become instructors. Of course, someone not open to new learning can expect nothing from us. As is well known, you can only learn what, deep down, you already know.

As you must realize, in the course of my six previous lives, I had been through hell and high water. Apprenticeship is no mean feat. In the hovels of destitute blacks of New Orleans I learned that love is more nourishing even than fresh fish, in Venice during the plague I learned to say goodbye to everything I called my own, in the yard of a juvenile correctional facility, I saw how much injustice is to be found inside justice. Pain—my own and that of others—made my fur molt. I've lost one eye and all of my self-respect over half a rotten sea bream.

I sacrificed half an ear to learn the true meaning of the popular saying "getting licked aside, we owed it to ourselves to fight." Obviously, I passed all tests with flying colors, because my sixth life landed me at London's National Library, if you don't mind. This was the equivalent of a jackpot in the karmic lotto. This was the sweet life, my dears, tailor-made for a culture vulture like myself. You can't possibly imagine the things I picked up for seventeen whole years pretending to be fast asleep on the reading tables, under the comfy warmth of the green lamps. Yes, I turned into a bookworm, my claws grew blunt and my teeth could no longer have sliced through live flesh but, in return, I gained the universe. (Credo Conclusively Proven and Absolute—Henceforth Meow No. 1234: You can't ever have it all. Not to be taken as self-evident, except by the obtuse.) I do declare that I would again choose the gift of knowledge a thousand times over. I suppose your god disagrees, but for myself, I side with Adam and Eve's daring. I am not saying that knowledge is a passport to paradise, but ignorance is surely hell.

I witnessed the eyes of thousands of readers sparkle as they leafed through the so-called books. I understood how humans, such silly and self-preoccupied animals, have wrested and maintained control over our planet: instead of transporting what they learned from body to body and mouth to mouth, they encased it in paper boats and sent those off to the four corners. Now, how brilliant is that? Einstein may be a bloated corpse by now, but he is still wandering about, analyzing his theories. And I swear to the tasty ocean shrimp, it's like he's lounging right there on the sofa and the two of you are chatting away for all you're worth.

I'm telling you, I adored those containers of human knowledge, got addicted to their smell and decoded their hieroglyphs, gladly paying the price in hard work. It was through them that I strolled on the Red Planet and counted its rings one by one. I learned the bouillabaisse recipe à la mode de Marseilles. I heard the shamans of the Mexican desert talk about the plant of power, Datura (Meow No. 3678: Off the record, blithe Westerners, I wouldn't recommend trying it. Power requires power and you don't have it. You would be doing yourselves grievous harm.)

Why cosmic fate should have sent me to complete my apprenticeship on this earth as the offspring of a hideous alley cat, I had no idea. Why my first sense impression should be the azaleas of the cat-loving madam Sweetie, I knew not. All I knew was that there was a reason. It was up to me to solve the riddle. Which meant I needed to be tuned in with eyes and ears wide open. Thankfully, I was a living testament to patience and persistence. I would suckle the unspeakable mother and then retire for hours on end to a strategic position behind the bushiest bush. I observed carefully. I diligently searched. Unfortunately, Madam Sweetie's garden wasn't Hyde Park or even your average neighborhood commons. Nicely turned out, well-kept lawn, flowerbeds and all that sort of thing, but, my dears, the place was deserted. Few came into that place and few came out. How on earth was the Ideal Parent pageant I had in mind going to happen? The truth is that, despite my inherent optimism, I was close to despairing for good and to attempting a move to a more suitable observation point, when, finally, the heavens (i.e. the garden gate) opened and in *they* walked!

My future family (and other animals)

He was Sweetie's one and only son—I knew it because the sweetness in her greetings would cause a diabetic to drop dead on the spot. I swear she gazed at him like Michelangelo would at his David. The young Mr. Ziggy was tall and lean (so lean, as a matter of fact, that I became concerned. Might there be a food shortage at their place? To check!) and the perfect gentleman. He spoke in a low voice, quietly and precisely—he would be a great success on radio. A man of internal combustion. He sat in his armchair and only got up when he needed to help his father carry a cooking grill. She, on the other hand, was also tall, but thankfully well padded, so, no need to fear a food shortage. (Next fear—she wouldn't be eating all there was and not sharing, would she? To check.) The Damsel in question wasn't merely the external combustion type. By the ocean shrimp, she wouldn't sit still, she was a live spinning top. You know the kind—one of those aficionados of the superlative, smoking with both hands, speaking in tongues, laughing up a storm and crying a river. OMG, the cyclone and its eye, I thought, with them barely settled on the straw furniture set up on the lawn. I liked it!

As it turned out, this was yet another of their traditional August evening family barbecues. The tables were laid out, the beers were set to cooling, the meats had been marinating since morning. Mr. Jean, Sweetie's husband since time immemorial, was a natural with all things manual. He was a great tinkerer. Hot-water heating, pipes, watering systems, broken roof tiles,

insulations, he could handle it all and handle it well. Above all else, though, his hands were partial to the grill. On that fateful day, then, he was organizing his much beloved cholesterol festival. Irresistible, yummy cholesterol hiding inside frankfurters and ribs and hams and hamburgers. The smell was making me swoon—it is a well-known fact that us felines need protein, a great deal of it. You can keep the courgettes and the tomatoes all to your healthy self, my vegetarian friends. We go after meat, whether red or white, and that is that. As such, we worship the Jeans of this world. If I could, I'd climb and park myself around his neck and be his fur collar for life. But I couldn't. I was all of six inches and still undercover. My mission took precedence.

So, then, I eavesdropped, my ears pricked to full capacity. Allow me to clarify. Not to hurt your feelings, but our hearing is a lot better than yours. We register differences of ⅕ and ¹⁄₁₀ in tone, whereas your rudimentary ear makes do with ¼. Truth be told, the snow-whites among us have a certain ear deficiency. Some of us are stone deaf, others half-deaf. But where I am concerned, there's no need for alarm. A grey mark over my left eye, the only blemish in my otherwise perfect whiteness, was testimony that my hearing was over twice as good as normal. I heard my personal god, Mr. Jean, complain about the inadequacy of the available lemons, I heard Sweetie pressuring everyone to have more cheese pie and, finally, I heard the visiting couple from the northern suburbs talk about books. Mind you, not books they had read but ones they had written! Hallelujah! Have the heavens rained breathing, living writers on my lawn?! I stretched out my ears like satellite dishes and distinctly heard the approaching footsteps of my destiny. That's right, that's what these folks were. Alright, my dears, don't get overexcited, they were no Burroughs or Plath. They had each recently published a book with children's stories and were congratulating each other over that. But that wasn't to be frowned on, either. I was no snob. This was most definitely better than nothing.

My Perfect Whiteness had never chanced upon a writer, in any of my lives. Just upon their books, was all. What kind of a job this was, how one went about it, I had no idea. On first sight, it did look like it served its purpose. My housemates-to-be (if you don't mind me jumping the gun here) evidently had time to spare, seeing they were parked on that lawn for 6-7 hours in high spirits, commenting on this and that and nibbling away at everything—of which there was an abundance, since they left at least five huge steaks completely unmolested. To be sure, there was the fear that they might belong to that category of intimidating writers who make up phrases like "the unbridled subjectivity of existence signifies the end of subjectivity," but I was determined to risk it.

This is your cue, I thought to myself. Luck helps the daring! I gave my fur the once-over, I carefully licked my hands, feet and tail, I put on my "gorgeous but ill-starred orphan" expression and I came out to adopt them. As I am no novice, I went straight for the most challenging target: Her.

SHE WAS A WOMAN WITH A PAST . . .

. . . but I wasn't going to let her past deprive me of my future. I may have easily fit in the palm of your hand, but I still had a few tricks up my sleeve (Meow No. 4567: Don't let yourselves be taken in by sniveling, my dears. No one is stronger than those who pose as weak.) Well, then, the first thing that Madam Sweetie announced while serving five different kinds of meat, spinach, and cheese pies, quiches Lorraine and potato salad with homemade mayonnaise as hor d'oeuvres, was that behind the azalea bush a cat (that must have been my mother) a very ugly looking one (most certainly my mother) had given birth to a batch of kittens. (A batch? How dismissive is that, especially when madam hadn't even laid eyes on me!?) The Damsel sprang to her feet but Sweetie held her back. "No-no-no, you mustn't go near that fiend," she admonished. "I take her food because I feel sorry for her, with her new litter and everything, and she hisses at me. If you touch one of the kittens she'll tear you to shreds!"

The Damsel sat back down and reached for a cheese pie. Oh hell, I swore under my breath. Damned gossip. Can you imagine her coming over to investigate the bushes? Do you realize what a glamorous impression my perfect whiteness would make, surrounded by three of nature's monstrosities? (Meow No. 987: The perception of reality is comparative. Dear Hephaestus, you mustn't go out in public next to Adonis, it shoots your chances down in flames.)

And then, at last, began the flow of valuable information. It was disclosed that the Damsel had never much liked cats. (But why, you nincompoop?) She always wanted a dog. (Oh dear! Please say you're not a petty tyrant looking for subjects!) But years ago, a cousin pretty much tricked her into taking a male striped kitten of unsurpassable charm for a week, for a month, "only temporarily until we find someone," in other words, for good. The infant was christened Zooey from the character in that novel by Salinger, a mysterious American Buddhist Jewish writer who lived as a hermit for fifty-five years driven by his fear of becoming well-known, with the result that he became even better known. (Meow No. 8643: Nothing worse than the fear of fear itself.)

At first, their relationship was the pits. The Damsel, prime minister and sole resident of her universe since forever, was at that time going through an "I-Don't-Give-a-Hoot" phase. She used the phrase as ammunition against all and sundry (parents, siblings, friends, boyfriends, colleagues, fellow passengers on the bus asking her to move forward a tiny bit), including the perfectly blameless. For his part, Zooey—I surmise in his second or third life—who sniveled all day and all night long to get her attention, merely managed to get on her nerves. It isn't hard for me to sympathize. Small wonder he couldn't fathom how he'd been expelled from the comfort of the cat-loving cousin's place and found himself in the mean apartment of this ice-cold maiden. Why must he hang from the tresses of the bedspread, trying to climb like a mountaineer up the Himalayas of her bed? Was he not entitled to a few inches atop the eiderdown? She said it was unhygienic. What the hell? He was not a slimy troll, he was just a baby with a little pink nose. Mind you, the word baby alone was enough to give the Damsel an allergic reaction. "The weight!" she intoned. "The responsibility!" "You aren't even free to die, if you're a parent!" "Who wants the commitment hanging over one's head?" Well, lady, you do have a touchy head and one that is easily breakable, too, it seems to me.

Just so you can appreciate what I was up against, I'm going to make a tiny leap to the future: As was amply proven during the first months of our life together, the Damsel thought the world of her head. She had made herself comfortable in there and refused to come out. She conceived and gave birth to thoughts, probable and improbable, she reared alternative selves, she spun plots, noted debts and underlined omissions, she set up court and issued convictions and acquittals, she regurgitated the past like a goat and stretched it to join the future, she jotted down possible versions, she applied pressure to make it grow more spacious so she could fit in it the whole factory where she constructed her similes and metaphors. No trust in the body whatsoever. A simple accessory. Feet for moving, hands for holding. A tool.

OMG, what a fool! "If I do end up adopting her, I'll have to start from scratch," I thought. "Open your arms. Well done, dear. This is called a hug. Very nice. A hug can save you seven thousand words. A good hug can replace every single acquittal issued by your mind-court. See what I mean? Well done, dear!" (Meow No. 667: The Damsel, like all lower mammals, responds well to a reward system.) Anyhow. I'm closing the parenthesis and getting back to the past that all but nearly wrecked my future.

Zooey was growing up, winning over friends of the Damsel, but never managing to win her over. On the other hand, though, she was a handy housemate. She never became cumbersome. She let you be. If you opt for the sad version, you might call that indifference. If you see it more positively—and Zooey seemed a positive lad—you'd call it liberalism. Naturally, she didn't have him castrated. Naturally, she allowed him to come and go into the street whenever he felt like playing the thug. Cat lovers were warning her that he'd get hooked to the street and would one fine day abandon home life to give himself wholly to the joys of tramping. She herself knew about tramping, knew its attraction. "He can please himself," she would say. "It's his life." (Meow No. 1996: if you discern too much liberalism in love, dears, then you are not loved, unless you are housemates with the Dalai Lama. Then again, there is the exceedingly rare case that you are in fact loved very veeery much . . .) Anyhow, the Damsel was not the Dalai Lama. What she wanted was to kind of be rid of him, really, via the liberal treatment. She had also foolishly believed all the nonsense in the yellow press, which dog lovers kept confirming: *Cats are indifferent to their owners, all they care about is their home ground and their comfort. Cats don't understand anything. They just look out for themselves.* Up yours, you derogatory cads. Everybody understands everything and so do we, in fact, even more so.

I wouldn't blame you if you wondered what possessed me, after hearing all this, to take it upon myself to get involved with Mrs. I-Don't-Give-A-Hoot. Just pace yourself. This was the introduction. Now, here comes the main subject. One fine day during the period in which the relationship between Zooey and I-Don't-Give-A-Hoot may by summarized as follows: "my cat comes in at 6.00 A.M. from the alley, goes straight to his dish, takes care of his hunger, his thirst, drops in for a meow by the desk where I'm sitting and then heads straight back out"; one day, all hell breaks loose. The weather in I-Don't-give-A-Hoot's life was tempestuous. She'd become embroiled in the madness of love with a guy who was fantastic but also every bit as mad as her, and there a fully-fledged war was being waged. They were victorious in turns but they shared the same Achilles' heel: the soft spot each had for the other weakened them and, in the end, turned their heads soft as well. They split up once, made up twice, split up three more times. They were on the heaven-to-hell express shuttle. That fatal afternoon, however, the shuttle had broken down in the pits of hell and the former lovebirds were in the middle of the main street, yelling at each other—what else?—IDON'TGIVEAHOOT!

After the ignominious end of hostilities, the Damsel crawled willy-nilly back to her pad, slammed the door behind her and settled under her eiderdown. This was her ritual therapy: every time her boat crashed against the rocks of reality, she hid in her bed, silently waiting for the warmth of the eiderdown to stave off the arctic cold.

She had spent over three hours in her assumed position of horizontal statue when Zooey traipsed into the room. It was his time. Hers was a small house, he was visible from all quarters. The dude came in through the open balcony door and stood still for a moment. He got wind of it straight off, something wasn't right. With a summary check, he saw I-Don't-Give-A-Hoot flat out like a fresh corpse; he then, for the first time, leapt without hesitation on the bed and sat in front of her face, looking concernedly into her eyes. "Zooey, go and eat," she stammered with difficulty. But Zooey didn't go to his food or to his drink. Even a naïve cat on its second-to-third life knows that there are moments destined to unfurl the grandeur that the paltry everyday leaves stagnating inside of you. If you let them pass by, you are an embarrassment to the species, better dead by far. So, Zooey stood his ground, in vigil to his pal, heedless of hunger and thirst. He was determined to become the fortification standing between her and the encroaching despair. Throughout the night he tirelessly trained on her his healing, anti-inflammatory gaze, until it was day and she got up to go to work. Mission accomplished, he told himself and devoured the can of tuna with peas that had been waiting for him since yesterday. I bet he felt nine feet tall and mightily accomplished. He had done his race justice. Not to mention that he had laid out the first carpet square for my arrival on the scene.

Between the steak and the beers, the cat talk had really gotten going among the group on the lawn. I was on full throttle myself. I was going all out to be adopted and that was that, wild horses wouldn't have kept me back. What I heard was enough and more than enough. Her cat experience to date may have been patchy and thin but it had a Hollywood ending with a moral lesson. My colleague Zooey had worked two miracles in one. He not only flabbergasted her with his sensitivity, he also rubbed her face into her own callousness.

There, then, was a Damsel who had been taught a good lesson, and in rough circumstances, too. She, therefore, wasn't likely to forget it anytime soon. She would never treat me as if I were a fluffy toy that happened to eat and shit without a battery. And she wouldn't be one of those weird aunties, either, who deify their cats and dogs past all reason, just because they dislike the human race across the board.

You see, I did have bitter experience with this particular brand of pathology. On my third life, cat karma had sent me to the luxury apartment of an aesthete, a Spanish tycoon in Malaga. I was then a girl and my name was Sacha because I was the spitting image of Colette's Russian blue cat. My deranged owner, who bought me from a pet shop specializing in pure-blooded royalties, enthroned me summarily in his home as his life partner, counselor and personal coach. About his children, his wife and his colleagues he couldn't care less. I and I alone was the apple of his eye. He let his workers starve to death but hired a Thai chef to cook the ocean king prawns with coconut milk that I liked. There was madness there, five fathoms deep, my dears. I would meow and an army of servants would rear up: one suggested clean water from alpine springs, the other smoked salmon with crabmeat, the third a fur toning massage. At first it destroyed my character. I turned fat, lazy and perverted. But then I clicked. That twisted soul could only relate to someone absolutely in his power. So I decided to teach him a little lesson and went into counterattack. He would stroke me and I would tear him to shreds. But his perversity was bottomless: the more I tore him up, the more he worshipped me. I was utterly disgusted. The worst of all was that for a decade, I had to listen to him advertise his sick devotion to me as proof of enormous sensitivity. Get away from me, you psycho. At ten years I had reached the end of my tether. Alright, dear universe, lesson duly noted: I will always make sure to look for what's hiding under the bed of unconditional adulation. Now, please allow me to get sick and die since that's the only way out of his clutches.

In any case, the past is past. There was the future to look after now. So, I took a deep breath, gave myself a pep talk— "Yes, you can, you know you've got it!"—and I walked on stage just at the moment when the entire group was turned in the direction of my hideout. I tried an elegant and self-confident walk but unfortunately, being still an infant, I ended tumbling along on the lawn. The fortunate part was that my Perfect Whiteness looked resplendent against the deep green grass.

The first to locate me was the weak link in the chain, Madam Sweetie.

"Ah, there it is, look, it's come out!" she cried out, clapping her hands like a sixty-year-old infant.

"Why, yes! Look at it run! But where is it heading to?" the others chorused.

The Damsel at long last put down her beer and focused on

the fuzzy ball hurtling toward her. The Japanese tactic of surprise attack was very much relevant to my purpose here. It doesn't pay to leave your target any time to respond. But then, I was a manga kitten in action: I accelerated madly and before she could move, I reached her shoes, stepped on them, and started climbing up her jeans. In zero time I was in her lap, where I feigned a fainting spell! (Meow No. 679: Dear Mohammed, don't kid yourself. The mountain isn't moving an inch. If you fancy a panoramic view, you'd better start climbing!)

The gathering was overcome by ripples of enthusiasm. A dozen hands were pulling at me from every direction but I was holding fast to my target's trousers and wouldn't budge. "Well, hey, I think it has adopted you," Madam Sweetie ascertained. The seated Damsel, naturally felt flattered. (Meow No. 98,765: Everybody goes nuts about feeling chosen. Otherwise, pray tell, why would they stand for hours outside the so-called clubs waiting for some muscled geek to pick them out from the hoi polloi and allow them to spend 500 euros on a bottle of suspect whiskey?)

She lifted me up to face level and looked into my eyes. "See that? One is green and the other one blue!" she announced. Thanks, dad, for making me special. I know all about human folly. They want their clothing to advertise its maker loud and clear, they want a car that proclaims to the world their financial well-being. Even those pretending to be above material goods, like the Damsel, are susceptible to prettiness. Which was a bit irksome, but what was I to do? I was looking to be adopted by an ordinary human, not a guru.

"Let me see," Ziggy then said. And as soon as he saw, "Hey, everyone, he is the spitting image of David Bowie" he summed up his description of me, and won me over once and for all. I knew I was flat-out lucky even if I had no idea who that David person was. I would find out soon enough, anyway. In the

future I would hear a thousand repeats of my man Ziggy playing *Rock and Roll Suicide* on his guitar and singing *Time takes
a cigarette* like there was no tomorrow, accompanied by the
Damsel.

MY MOTHER'S SIN

Only, of course, no miracle lasts for more than three days. Madam Sweetie may have outdone herself in persuasiveness ("You're not leaving this fluff ball behind? This cutie pie? You don't have the heart, surely?"), Mr. Jean may have been supportive, Ziggy may have been virtually ready to give in, but the Damsel, though clearly she could not get her eyes and hands off me (And how could she? no, not little delectable me!) was being recalcitrant and kept repeating the hateful words, "No can do, absolutely no, not after what happened with the last one, we have sworn we'd never get another animal." (Now, dear, if you say "animal" in that tone of voice one more time, I'm going to really hit the roof. You mean you are not an animal yourself? Are you not animate? Or have you kicked the bucket and you're keeping it a secret?)

"Why, what did happen with the last one?" asked a neighbor who had meanwhile joined the party.

And, then, my dears, the bomb dropped: "We killed Boston," the couple murmured in unison, going red and green at the same time. On their foreheads a neon sign started flashing that said: GUILTY WITH NO EXTENUATING CIRCUMSTANCES.

I really didn't need to hear that. I was dumbfounded, let me tell you. This was the surprise of all surprises. My hairs stood on end. I was a seventh life cat: how could I have been that far off the mark? Soon enough, however, my peace and calm were restored. As I heard the Damsel confess, Boston was the name they'd given to a pretty colleague of mine that her beau had given her as a gift when she deigned to come back after several months' sabbatical in Boston. They had loved Boston and had made her a proper member of the family. Thanks be to Zooey who had prepared the ground. No more of the single girl's one-hour stands with Zooey. They were now an item and fully prepared to give their cat a proper home. Between us, deep down, way deep, Ziggy might have hoped that, by making her a cat mom, she would gradually come to terms with the "terrible responsibilities" and the "unbearable burden" of a two-legged baby. Madam Sweetie who was mad keen on grandchildren, was most certainly hoping that Boston would work a miracle in that direction. As it turned out, the only children Boston brought to the house in the end were her own: Texas, New York, Philadelphia, (North) Carolina and California—all so adorable, thankfully, that homes were found for them on the spot.

The climax came when Ziggy finally talked the Damsel into buying a house of their own. The timing was perfect: their last landlady, a centurion with a plastic kneecap, mad as a hatter, had, after the first month, started sending them eviction notices and calling the police. She believed that an infernal machine they kept in their house was recording her conversations in an effort to drive her insane. The old girl didn't need any such machine, of course, she was already far gone! So, they packed and left after the tenth eviction notice hoping at least to remain compos mentis themselves.

They moved into a delightful little house near a wooded hill, thinking they'd hit the jackpot. Fat chance! The new landlady had an acute ownership complex: She barged in whenever she pleased to check if they'd hung any pictures on the walls, or whether they were destroying her floors with their dancing. Eventually, she announced to them out of the blue that her daughter had gotten married which, in effect, was a marching order. The Damsel was beside herself with nerves. "You can stuff your private properties and your weddings," she kept saying. "Tell me that I'm wrong to detest them!"

I need at this point to share with you another one of her great fixations, which gave her poor other half much grief. It wasn't only children that, to her, were a ball and chain, but private property as well. Any kind of private property. For instance, I bet not even Lenin's daughter hated private cars like she did. "A thousand times better a bus or a train," she'd say. "I don't get sworn at by other drivers and I don't have to fret over a parking space. I can read my book, listen to my music, and arrive wherever I'm going, calm and collected." Naturally, she had ruled out country houses as well. ("They are a form of slavery. You stay rooted in one spot.") She didn't even want an ordinary house for her own. ("It's a nuisance. And it's boring. I prefer getting to know the neighborhoods and houses of other people."). For the first decade of her adult life she moved every year, like a Palestinian refugee. Except, the more the books multiplied and the harder the boxes became to shift, the longer the periods became during which she could stay put. (Meow No. 980: Ideology may be radical, but reality is more radical still.) She got to a point of spending two and three years in the one house. But when she fell for Ziggy she put her foot in it, as the saying goes, without even realizing it. He was a homebody, with none of her gypsy leanings. And beware of homebodies—they'll find a way of turning you into one as well; and you'd better be grateful for it! (As a matter of fact, she's still thanking him. She loved that house so much that, for the first time, she used the word "my" next to the word "house." She discovered how sweet that "my" could be. And once that starts to happen, you know as well as I do that, afterwards, the sky's the limit.)

So, they leafed through the classifieds and found an amazing place in the northern suburbs. Its view of the sunset would be the envy of the aficionados of Santorini. It was like a ship, open and breezy from all sides. Not to mention that right next door lived Polyxeni, a dyed-in-the-wool cat lover with seventeen cats inside the house and innumerable others galli-vanting in the sixteen hectares of her orgiastic garden. The birds sang in the trees and they meowed underneath. It was heaven. The folks got all excited, they painted it and fixed it up and then brought in all of their furniture, books and CDs in one day. They let Boston wait at the house by the wooded hill until it was all set up, so she could walk into her new kingdom and find it all spruced up and brand new. So, when they drove back to the old place to pay the landlady the final rent, they asked for the cat to stay in the empty house for a couple of hours, so they could nip downtown and buy new handles for the kitchen cupboards. But the petty-minded ignoramus put her foot down and demanded that they take Boston with them, thinking—would you believe it!?—that they might take off and just abandon her there. The Damsel, who was congenitally averse to human stupidity, grabbed poor Boston up and damned the despicable wrench to hell for thinking she could behave toward a living being as if it was a stool with a broken leg. The problems were: a) they had no cat basket to transport Boston; and, b) the cat was not in the least fond of being moved around, so (the stupid, unthinking) retards found no better solution than to put her in the trunk. The trip wasn't long but, alas! It was long enough to turn the trunk into a death chamber. Boston suffered heat-stroke and expired on the kitchen tiles of her new home, which was destined to be mine. Sorry, Boston, that's the name of the game: Your death, my life.

The burden of their guilt blighted the joy of the house that was like a ship. They used to dream of her as she lay breathless on the tiles, with them trying in vain to reverse the damage by applying cold compresses. They damned the landlady, her daughter, their stupidity, their own temper, the cupboard handles. But what was done was done. And the only true punishment they could impose on themselves would be never again to get a cat, since they were incapable of protecting it.

AND WHAT FAULT IS IT OF MINE, DAMSEL?

I listened to her tale and it gave me goose bumps. Yes, they're only human, imperfect creatures, prone to making mistakes. What scared me the most was the guilt dripping from every word, every stare, every grimace they made. I had peeled my eyes and pricked my ears trying to get a handle on them now that I hardly knew a thing about them. (Meow No. 987: The more you know about someone, the more confused you get. It's the truth: You know best the one you don't know at all.) I had learned to fear guilt even more than stupidity. The dumb person might make a middling go of things, but the guilt-ridden is sure to fuck up, precisely because of their guilt. In my fourth life I'd seen a man go under because of his guilt over drinking himself to oblivion and harassing his children. To bear the burden of that guilt, he drank even more until he became a burnt-out alcoholic with his liver shot to pieces. Which is why I'm saying: Guilt is a sly one—you start out feeling sorry for your kids' not having a proper father and you end up making them fatherless.

And that is exactly how the couple before me were feeling: they were contemplating taking a cat under their care precisely because they felt guilty for not having been able to care for a cat! Go on, you inconsequential creatures, stop deliberating, I was telling them with my tail. It is destined for us to be house-mates, make up your mind and get this over and done with! I needed a writer to compile the bon mots of my feline wisdom and I got me two. Come to think of it, Bukowski would have been the ideal candidate! He wouldn't think twice about it. He'd keep me better than his paramours. Not to mention he'd write my memoirs in English and I'd become an international bestseller, not just a third rate novella for local consumption . . . Ah well . . . Be that as it may, at that given moment, I was gazing upon the freshly mown lawn, while our good man Charles was under it.

"Come now, just take a look at him, he's such a darling. Look how he's watching you with those bright little eyes . . . You don't have the heart to leave him, surely?"

You got it right. Night was coming on and my eyes sparkled as I gazed up at her like she was the center of my existence, and nobody in the whole wide world is indifferent when faced with a pair of eyes in love. (If she knew the first thing about cats, she would know that we have a kind of mirror-like layer on our eyes, the so called *tapedum lucidum*, which reflects the light so we can see better in the dark. But she didn't, a fact which allowed any number of interpretations to bloom unchecked in my favor.)

With a little bit of help from looking through the eyes of love, from my irresistible beauty and from the insistence of my bleeding heart advocate, Madam Sweetie, I won the battle. My gumption at so speedily putting myself forward to win a woman's heart gave me my name: they called me Zach, after a bon vivant of Athens, a well known socialite and famous womanizer. A few months later I had won myself an additional appellative: Sugar. No need for comment here, I was simply as sweet as they come.

THEIR HOME, MY SWEET HOME

They took me home wrapped in a red scarf like an Easter bunny. As soon as I set foot in the hall, I felt that this was my turf. This was where I'd build my kingdom. It belonged to me and I to it. But since the human couple living there before me also surely possessed the proverbial grandiosity of their species, I couldn't afford to waste any time. I needed to make my terms perfectly clear right from the beginning. Because, my friends, as Meow No. 3456 will reveal, the deck is stacked right at the start. The casting of roles in the play to be enacted takes place very early on—one needs, therefore, to be vigilant . . .

First of all, I went about the place scouting. The house would prove more forthcoming than either of my new housemates. I sniffed out every inch of the bedroom: The books had long overflowed from the bookshelves and were scattered in profusion on dressers and on the floor. On her side, especially, a red dresser like a piece of kindergarten furniture was packed with two or three piles of unread books: It was her mini bookshop from which she nightly chose a reading that suited her mood.

I noted with interest that the Damsel had converted the spare (and ideally isolated) room into an office for herself, leaving Ziggy to set up his writer's nest in a corner of the (actually fairly large) living room next to the stereo and across from the TV. I struggled to decide whether she was being unfair to him or whether she was indulging him. I never did manage to settle that particular question. Ziggy proclaimed himself hard done by but, on the other hand, I saw how he itched to listen to this or that piece of music or steal a look at the television. "I write about the cinema and television," he'd argue. "I need to know what is on." As you might guess, he was having himself on. He shared that particular defect with me: He loved to waste time. In the mornings, he made his coffee, turned on the PC and played Tetris for about an hour, as a warm-up. After that, he played a few games of patience for good luck, answered his emails, made some more coffee because he was done with the first one and then he started thinking about how on earth to begin the first chapter of his first novel. Just as he became lost in contemplation, the rival thought would occur to him that he had a deadline to meet for his first script which meant he needed to stop thinking about his novel at once and start thinking about the script. He experienced a significant bout of stress. To counter it, he played another game of Tetris. Humans are an intriguing species and writers even more so. I still wonder where so many well turned out phrases managed to fit in among all the Tetris blocks.

To be sure, with time I understood what the devil it was he liked about that game. Managing to fit the colored blocks in the available spaces in the time allotted gave, him a temporary sense of orderliness. If they found their places, so too would his life: the scripts would be delivered on time, his ideas about novels would turn out to be great successes. In the meantime, he postponed for the time being the hardest test: turning into reality what his imagination had envisioned. Because reality does have that one damn disadvantage: It always ends up less. And it is paralyzingly real.

The Damsel was of a different variety. When she had to write, she wrote. She sat her ass down and applied herself, as the expression goes. She sat in front of the screen and pressed the keys. An exemplary worker of the alphabet. She wasn't enough of an imbecile to allow herself to be paralyzed by the thought that her novel wasn't *The Idiot*. (Besides, Dostoyevsky himself didn't know that he would be writing *The Idiot* when he was writing *The Idiot*—not that she was such an imbecile as to think that she would someday write *The Idiot*.) So, then, she focused on one target and pursued one thread. She didn't answer any phone calls, she didn't pay any visits, she didn't entertain irrelevant thoughts. She only got up for the fridge, the bathroom and the coffee machine. As you gather, dears, crazy things happened in this house. The inside turned the outside inside out. The sitting Ziggy turned into a spinning top and the Spinning Top stayed glued to her chair until she'd made it through her daily schedule. And, naturally, each fought the other's habit. Every so often, she would delete from his hard disk the damn games; he would invade her office at intervals and say to her, "Come now, let's take a coffee break, you hard-boiled protestant, talk to me a little, you factory worker." They were fun.

You could see why they were together; it made perfect sense. Opposites attract, it's common knowledge—especially if deep down they are actually the same. Those two, at all events, had achieved a kind of balance. It was now up to me, as a new member, to infiltrate the balance of the household and give it a new twist in my favor, without unbalancing it. First of all, I needed to set it out perfectly clear right from the start that I was no pet, I was a housemate with equal rights. Particularly, that is, the Damsel who had a sad record on the matter, from what I overheard. *Tu casa es mi casa, senora.* If you harbor the illusion that you can imprison me in a room or a balcony, then you are gravely deluded. Because I am here in order to teach you to share. Unfortunately for you, you have still to cotton onto the fact that I am a wise teacher in his seventh life disguised in a two-month-old fur ball, or else you wouldn't have let me into your castle so easily. You see, my dears, human beings are incredibly attached to their foibles. I hate hairs, says the lady. So, what of it? And I hate seeing you smoke like a chimney but I don't make an issue of it, as deleterious as it is to my health. Did you hear me comment on it? Did I make any faces? Did I meow disconcertedly? No, I accepted it. You have some small parts that I adore, other small parts that compel my interest, ones that bore me, and you have some small parts that I detest as much as water on my pelt. The sum total, nevertheless, is you, and it's you I have chosen; therefore, all those parts too. Now, why do you insist on putting me on a butcher's block and cutting me up into fillet and mince? I am here, in front of you, all of me, and I am going to teach you to either love the other person as a whole or, finally, retreat into the wilderness like the Prophet Elias, because only those who aspire to sainthood are so selfish!

And the struggle was under way! The Damsel's first move was to close the door of the hall which divided the house in two. I was overcome with shock and awe. Heeeeeey! We cats hate doors, didn't she know that? No matter how philosophical I tried to be, it was impossible to stomach the fact that I was under house detention in one half of the apartment, which someone more superficial than me might have called a paradise: The kitchen with the treats, the living room with the fluffed up pillows and the fireplace, the veranda with the flowerpots and the view to Madam Polyxeni's cat kingdom. Yet this sly female intended to cut me out of her more personal spaces: Her bedroom and her office. Meaning, where she thought, where she wrote and, most important, where she slept and dreamt.

I imagine you are familiar with the age-old tradition of my species: a cat never ever sleeps with its back turned to someone. Especially during our first lives, when we like to advertise our smartness and savvy, we are constantly on the alert. Don't let it fool you that we roll on our backs leaving our tummies exposed. Our four well-armed paws are always in warlike readiness. The slightest suspect move will result in prompt laceration. If we do fall asleep with our back to someone, it means we are giving them the highest acknowledgement in terms of trust and selfless love. I had in mind to offer that acknowledgement but also, mind you, to receive it! I knew it wasn't going to be at all easy but a seventh-life cat disdains what is easy. Damsel, it might take me the fifteen or twenty years that I have available but I, Sugar Zach, will eventually tame you!

WOLF IN SHEEP'S CLOTHING

No sardonic smiles, if you please. I know what I'm talking about. We domesticated you, you highfalutin species, not you us. Your delusion that you are masters of the universe has become plain ridiculous, already. Let's get this straightened out once and for all: Our forefathers derive from the early mammals that survived mighty dangerous conditions and did so better than even the high and mighty dinosaurs, precisely thanks to the sharpness of their wits. That, my dears, is called adaptability. Not meaning to brag but my family tree is full of stars: I have jaguars, I have leopards, I have panthers, I have pumas—what don't I have! All you have is a bunch of apes—nothing you would call a *libro d'oro*, really.

You might well ask what possessed us, indomitable felines, to get involved with the likes of you. It doesn't have to do with love, I'm afraid, as much as with need. My great great grandmothers in Northern Africa made the decision to approach you seven thousand years ago, not because they admired your "civilization," but because that way they could get a meal with less toil and less risk. In Egypt, you see, humans had learned how to cultivate crops and the mice were holding feasts in their storehouses. They'd hidden in there and were gnawing away day and night, undisturbed. Mice, though, were in turn our mainstay, so our grandmothers smelt them and they were tempted. The more sensible ones were intimidated and didn't dare come close to the human settlements. Better safe than sorry, they thought. But the less inhibited and daring started slowly to converge on the storehouses. Whoever's on the prowl gets more variety out of life, they figured. So they storm the mice party, get their fill and get a taste for the easy life. Having it easy is no small thing, my dears—it changes you into a different kind of cat!

There were, however, reciprocal benefits. You found us quite handy yourselves. Smoothly and inexpensively, you got rid of the rodents fouling your crops. Well, these were the lines along which the marriage took place, like all marriages: A contract based on mutual advantage. Every so often, we would give a demonstration of fetching and depositing at your feet a rat or a snake, just so you knew how conscientious we were about our duties and would not drive us away from the storehouse feast. It was kind of fun, and the reflex that some blue-blooded cousins exhibit, when, on occasion, they present their housemates with a dead cockroach, making them wonder whatever possessed that chic pet to make such unappetizing presents, dates from precisely that period.

So, then, my dears, slowly and unobtrusively we eventually managed to occupy your homes. In the beginning, we only came in to hunt the mice and then went back out to the beat. Fast food may be nice but roaming the streets and fields is in our blood. However, the cities you've managed to create, which are nothing short of purgatories, have made things rather tough. If we roam those battlefields freely our life expectancy is no more than a couple of years. Cars run us over, we get intentionally poisoned by unbalanced characters, bullies torture us for sport. You call all that kind of thing an advance in civilization! We, nevertheless, happen to be realists. If the outside is a living hell, then we make sure we have access to the inside. That is how we end up in the safety of your living rooms. And you now openly plead with us to accept living alongside you. On occasion you pay good cash to own us. Nowadays, you kill mice and cockroaches by yourselves with sprays, only you have an even bigger problem. You have made your life unlivable. You subvert, badmouth and abuse one another. You've become suspicious. You are scared to stroke humans in case they bite your arm off. You are friendless. And, thus, you have need of us. Whereas we once approached you for food, now you beg us for some sustenance for your deprived soul. You will do anything for a caress that doesn't involve risk.

But let's not kid ourselves, all things have a price. From the moment we turned exclusively into salon pets, we also turned into wusses. A huge part of our intelligence disappeared along with our enemies. (Meow No. 562: Enemies keep you in shape. So, don't complain if your good luck is up. It's highly likely that it's thanks to this very fact that you are still on your feet.) If you aren't on tenterhooks about where the next disaster is coming from, you don't have adrenaline enough to keep you vigilant. Likewise with camouflage. What do you need swift reflexes for, when you are cozily ensconced in the Damsel's arms, fast asleep? Is the tuna going to try and escape from the tin can, for you to chase after it?

Do you now see, my dears, how I, the proud feline, found myself in the position of claiming my rights as a housemate to all of her domicile (pardon me, *our* domicile)? Now, she, herself, needs to understand that she ought to spend time with me in order to be able to properly write down my story. I am in no mood whatsoever to be the lead in one of those saccharine pulp fictions that come a dime a dozen.

WAR IS THE FATHER OF ALL THINGS

I don't mean to brag but I happen to be a very methodical cat. An expert in warfare. As such, I decided to prioritize my aims. Number one was, of course, the door to the hall, that despicable construct designed by humans to carve up their vital space so as to create the illusion of independence. Forgive me, Damsel, but if you expect a door to make you independent, you are pitiful . . . May I also remind you that your vital space is also my vital space. I am therefore obliged to declare your move a *casus belli* and declare war forthrightly.

But let me take this from the beginning. The first day, you see, my dears, I was taken aback to see her leave the kitchen where they were having breakfast, saying to her beau, "I'm going to write now." At last, we're getting down to work, I thought, and happily followed her. As soon, however, as madam saw me following her, she pulled a sour face, ran off and closed the hall door behind her. I was left frozen on the spot, looking alternately at him and at her door. "Never mind her, Zach, come over here," Ziggy told me. I was such a wreck that the kind fellow took pity on me. He put me on his lap, gave me some milk for breakfast (with no preservatives, if you don't mind) and then let me explore the pillow heaven in the living room. But it was eating at me. I had a mission, I couldn't afford to waste my time. So I took up position next to the door in the hall. I felt weak and small. I didn't yet have a whole lot of ammunition available. So, I sought refuge in the weaponry of the weak: sniveling. I meowed insistently and cried for hours in front of the hateful door. I couldn't get my head around such coarseness. Didn't this woman know that we are sensitive to a fault? That we get anxious even if you change the brand of our cat litter? That if we lose someone close to us, we are adversely affected to the point where we are at risk of dying ourselves? Did she not appreciate that hapless me had left all relatives behind for the privilege of ascending to her fifth floor? These were the thoughts going through my head as I lay there wailing and drenched in my own tears.

And the sum total of my efforts? A big, fat, round zero! The Damsel was stewing so thoroughly in her own creative juices that it didn't even cross her mind to spare any time for me. The only thing she did was to cry out every so often from a distance, "Shut up, little Zach, you're being a royal pain!" It was a bitter new knowledge, acknowledging her writerly disdain for everything that didn't directly relate to her own interests.

I also realized that for the time being, our relationship was awfully unequal: She was a meter and seventy one centimeters tall and I was a dwarf. She can avail herself of words in which to frame her arguments at great speed ("I need to concentrate, Zach, enough with your mewling in my ear already. I'm going to throw you out, I'm warning you. You're going out on the veranda. I said, shuddup!") and I only have a "meow" to express a thousand words. Let it be noted that our forefathers in the jungle didn't utter a single sound. They went about their business haughty and silent. Ever since getting involved with you humans, we too started waffling on and meowing redundantly. But that isn't enough, either, because apart from being thick, humans are also tone-deaf and can't figure fundamental nuances such as between an "I'm-scared" meow and an "I'm-hungry" meow.

What with one thing and another, I got stubborn. What I lacked in size I made up in brains. And, Damsel, beware of smart cats. A colleague of mine who lived with the deceased novelist E.H. Gonatas had evolved to the point of lifting the lid from the pot, stealing the chicken that was cooking and then replacing the lid to avoid detection! I wasn't far behind that. I would observe and I would figure out how that devilish construct worked.

Now I am going to stoop low and gossip a little because she's irritated me. The Damsel was so dumb that, though we lived together for a full fifteen years, she never did realize just how smart I really was. Only after I was dearly departed did she come across an article in one of those cat magazines titled *How clever is you cat?* and she started grading me by assigning 1 to 10 to the following phrases:

My cat is independent and can look after himself. (Sure I am, but be careful: That doesn't mean you can abandon me to my own devices!)

My cat tries to influence me in order to get what it wants. (You can't imagine to what extent!)

My cat shows an interest in everything. (This is a seventh-life cat we're talking about, Damsel. It goes without saying that I am interested in everything. From the way ants toil to the reactions of the cornered mouse. Everything, all things, all the time.)

My cat understands my feelings and my reactions and responds to them. (You, on the contrary, don't have a clue about its feelings, you thick-skinned brute!)

My cat is self-confident and self-assured around house visitors. (Words are redundant. I'm not called Zach for nothing. The man I was named after was as worldly as they get.)

My cat recognizes its name and comes when I call him. (Even when I was having my favorite catnaps in my favorite flowerpot, I would jump to it like a skittish recruit as soon as I heard you call out—that's how stupid I was!)

My cat can solve a variety of problems, such as opening a drawer. (Why, yes, my dear. Which is precisely why that door of yours is not going to stand in my way!)

I got a total of seventy points which meant that, according to the specialist, I was a genius. Except, you, Damsel, weren't. You don't call someone clever who needs a specialist's certificate in order to understand their mate.

End of gossiping session. Return to action: I spent a great many working hours snivel-meowing before her closed door, checking: a) how long she could take my persistence; and, b) how exactly that thingamabob works called a door handle. Soon enough I got it. You needed to exert some pressure on one end of the handle in order to open the door. As you well know, I possessed no hand. Nor did I possess the necessary height to reach the handle and push it down with my paw. What was there left to do? Gain some speed, leap and throw all of my weight on the end of the handle. YES!YES!YES! That's it, I got it, I'm a Nobel candidate! So I did gather speed and I did leap, but it was all in vain, dears. I fell flat on my face without even getting as high as half a meter. I was still a baby, god damn it to hell! I needed more centimeters before I could leap to that height. And I needed more weight in order to push down on the handle effectively. Which is to say, I needed time to grow. In the meantime, I would restrict myself to weapon number one: sniveling. It was easier now, because my entire body hurt from throwing myself around. One thing, though, was for sure: There are some who, when defeated, will not fight again, so as not to be defeated a second time. Well, I wasn't one of those.

FOOD FOR THOUGHT

Hours went by, days went by, months went by, waiting. I ate my food passionately because I was in a hurry to grow up, with the end result being that I grew fat and greedy. But let me take things from the beginning.

I discovered that the Damsel was fiercely devoted to cooking. She kept bringing in weird contraptions (a wok from China, a bamboo-shoot steamer from the Philippines, a crepe-maker from Paris and so on). She also collected exotic condiments in her travels (chili and mole from Mexico, garam masala from India, green curry from Thailand, charissa from Morocco. Every so often, she would find a pretext to invite friends over for a meal. (I finished the article I was writing, it's Mahatma Gandhi's birthday, it's the spring equinox today, and suchlike.) While she owned a huge collection of gourmet recipe books, arranged on a kitchen bookshelf, she rarely made use of them. At most, she might steal a glance to get the general idea and after that, she pretty much did whatever came into her head. Improvisation upon improvisation. Some outcomes were happy, others of her experiments committed suicide inside the pot.

To be frank, I was very much impressed by the unheard of trouble humans took over their meals. Our forefathers, sober minimalists that they were, taught us that to keep ourselves alive, we require meat. So, then, as soon as hunger strikes, we go on the beat, hunt for the prey, tear it apart, sate our hunger and that is it. If we get hungry again, we just go back out.

Nature, see, has blessed us with living in the present. Whereas you, stuck in the past and therefore unceasingly anxious about the future, are unaware of the redeeming freedom of the present tense. I am hungry, therefore, I hunt and eat, is what we say. Keep things simple. I will be hungry again, given that I was hungry before, so I will need to make provisions as I am very much afraid of going without in the future, is what you say. (Oh dear, just writing this down made me all anxious!)

So you started storing food at a feverish pace for afterwards and for after afterwards. You built storehouses and you heartlessly imprisoned sheep, cows, chicken and pigs so you'd have them at your disposal. You stuffed them with garbage to fatten them quickly and cheaply. And here are the sad consequences: Sixty-seven million animals slaughtered yearly so that you can grow fat, dears. You don't even let the fish be. A trillion murdered in your frying pans each year unfailingly! The richest amongst you have developed even kinkier vices—you indiscriminately gnaw through everything: horses, frogs, sharks, reindeer. You will not desist even before species threatened with extinction. We are more merciful. I, myself, took into my protection an animal facing extinction, an old homeless guy who found shelter by reading in the public library. You, I am afraid, would gladly shoot him, if there weren't the legal consequences to reckon with.

And worst of all? During breaks, to lighten your chronic anxiety, you grab your rifles and go murdering in cold blood thousands of partridges, hares and wild boar, for your entertainment. Yours alone, as we are not in the least entertained.

Admit it, my dears: Abundance hasn't done you any good. You started out by cooking meat so that it would be better digested and you ended up marinating it in truffle oil and papaya seeds to then simmer in a wok, with baby corn and Asian bean shoots. Oh please! I mean, will you get over yourselves already!

Pardon me, I got carried away. What I meant to state was the following: you'd expect that with the Damsel's constant preoccupation with cooking, I would have eaten like a king. Hardly! You couldn't touch her concoctions! I needed meat and she prepared tortillas with guacamole. Thank you kindly, madam, but I'll pass!

She asked the doctor (unfortunately she had a useless one, the kind that winds up a vet after failing to become a proper doctor) who happily recommended that I only eat canned and dry cat food. "Only there will your kitty find all the necessary vitamins," he declared. Is that so? Then why don't you also restrict yourself to canned fish instead of ordering fresh sea bass on the grill? Anyway, the point is that financial interests, ignorance and lassitude drove me into the unhealthy embrace of the industry that was going to kill me slowly and pleasurably. Thankfully, the housemates were no misers. They bought for me the top gourmet canned goods: tuna, rabbit with vegetables, duck pâté, and my all-time favorite, ocean shrimp with trout. That once brought down the wrath of the Damsel's mother who went haywire as soon as she found out the price of the can: "People are going hungry out there and you're feeding this mongrel ocean shrimp?" she said, piqued. (Whom are you calling a mongrel, missus? God keep me from opening my mouth.)

The Damsel, on the contrary kept feeding me all the time. She liked big fat cats. Quite fat ones. Bear cats. So, she made me fat and then that's what she called me. ("Come here, fatso! Don't step on my tummy, fatso! You've put even more weight on, fatso!" and so on and so forth.) Poor innocent, she had no idea that she was digging her own grave. One fine morning, at the exact moment when the lady retired into her private quarters, closing the hated door behind her, I marshaled all of my eight kilos and leapt at the door handle. Following the thump of my body's impact, the handle bent, the locking mechanism released and the door to paradise opened at last. She got up from her desk gawping in amazement, grabbed me and threw me straight out again, murmuring, "You rascal, fatso." In vain, of course. Whether you like it or not, dearest, *Carthago delenda est*!

THE CAT AS MUSE IS A FIB

According to my calculations, I must have thrown myself upon the hateful door handle at least eighty-seven times. The Damsel met my willfulness with equal amounts of her own. "Go away, you, what's it this time! Can't you see I'm writing?" she would yell, and throw me out again. (It really made me wonder, hadn't she be told by any of her colleagues that the cat is the writer's muse? Is it possible she could be so uninformed?) She would chuck me out, back in I would sneak. Let's see who manages to wreck the other's nerves first, mademoiselle. Finally, the two of us combined did the door in. The handle came unstuck, the hinges loosened and a peace treaty was signed, confirming my victory. It was the happiest day of my life. The Damsel was writing away, wrathful, and I was urgently looking for a way to get introduced into her book. My theory was that this was a job to be accomplished in stages. First, I would enter as a secondary character in one of her books at least, then start upgrading until I became the lead hero in my own memoirs. Fiendish, no?

For a start, I stuck my mug right next to the keyboard. I spent endless hours at just that spot. Our working days started at about twelve in the morning (middle of the day, for others) and ended at about five in the morning. Fairly quickly I understood why writers and cats were an item, as the saying goes. Because they were *una faccia una razza*.[1]

---

[1] Translation from Italian: "Same face, same family." Common saying, originating with fascist theories of nationalist purity; today, it simply denotes a high degree of similarity manifested in looks and mannerisms.

To make my meaning plain: They sit as we do, for hours and hours on end in the same spot, unmoving, unspeaking, undoing. They are thinking, they claim. I very much doubt it. I think that they eventually get abstracted from all the thinking and fall asleep inwardly, the way we do. I don't want you to misunderstand me, I count this in their favor. Doing nothing is, in all seriousness, one of the hardest things in the world. Plato and Aristotle even pointed out to their students that the principle of nonaction is one of the most spiritual in the world.

They are loners and misanthropes. They want their peace and quiet and so do we. They keep you at a distance and they come to you only when they choose. We aren't accountable to anyone as a matter of course. They, for their part, merely throw out the phrase "I'm working now" and they are done. In actual fact, of course, they may be contemplating the possibility of whether their current significant other is cheating on them.

Their schedule is deranged and incoherent. Every normal person gets up in the morning, goes to work, comes back, has lunch, engages in some form of recreation and as soon as it is night, they go to sleep. Not so with writers. They wake up at any time, they eat whenever, they have their fun and games no matter when and at nights, they circulate sleepless, like ghosts (some in bars and nightspots, some at their office). It's quiet at night, they say, and you have a better chance of working. Ergo . . . ! We are nocturnal animals, as everyone knows. We are mightily in favor of you also burning the midnight oil, so that there's some activity on, no matter if everyone else thinks of you as good-for-nothing scroungers.

They are curious and observe everything, just like we do. We merely keep our conclusions to ourselves. (When the Damsel speaks on the phone, she gets irritated. Therefore, it's better if I don't even go near her as soon as I hear the phone ringing.) They record theirs and then sell them off as products of their imagination.

They spend a lot of time at home. The saying "My home is my castle" was made up with them in mind. We do likewise. Once we claim a spot for ours, wild horses can't move us. What are we, crazy, to mill about in the cold and damp? In the blazing sun and the smog?

They are usually too self-absorbed to notice a thing. They seem to be there but they're really not. They let you be. I, personally, have taken a crap—if you'll pardon my language—in seven flowerpots, clawed to shreds the red leather armchair in the living room and torn up endless kitchen paper rolls, completely undisturbed. When the Damsel gets up from her desk and I fear my trespasses will be found out, I merely hide under the couch until her swearing subsides along with the hurtling in my direction of slippers and assorted petty objects. I then emerge, as winsome and charming as ever. Nothing lasts, my dears. Thankfully, that goes for her anger as well. When you, egocentric creatures, become self-absorbed, that's the end of that. Only, there is a dark side to this. Not even a fire brigade siren can rouse you. Experience has taught me there are two approaches to getting the attention I want when I want it: Either pretend to be nice and cute, which is boring and slightly demeaning, or become a menace, which is easy and pleasant, though unfortunately, risky. For the sake of a well-rounded education, I have ended up alternating the two.

The issue was that the Damsel seriously made up her mind to ignore me, which severely hampered my mission. Whether I was in her office or not, it was all the same. In the beginning, I impersonated a beguiling feline. I laid myself out at a strategic position next to the keyboard and yawned, meaning: I'm settled just fine, your ladyship, you just go on with your business and never mind me. After some time passed and I saw she was ignoring me, I moved my paw a little to the left, coming dangerously within range of her field of action. She pushed me away. In five minutes I moved it again, reaching a few cen-

timeters farther than the last time. I was overcome by anxiety. How on earth would I ever manage to get in her book? Should I possibly touch the keyboard? As soon, however, as I dared touch one of the keys, a redundant A appeared on the screen. "Aaaah! What have you done, you fat monster! I'm going to throttle you!" she screamed. She grabbed me and threw me on the floor without as much as blinking. This is a sorry state to be in, Zach, old boy, I thought, meowing dispiritedly. What gall she has to humiliate your Perfect Whiteness in such a manner! What importunity, dashing you from the pristine heights to ground level.

I decided, nevertheless, to temporarily make peace with my debased status. A question of strategy, my dears. I ascertained on that occasion that the carpet was thick and blue, pretty much the color of my right, and prettier, eye. I made myself comfortable on her right foot. It was warm and it was bare—thankfully, as I detest shoes. "Get away from there, silly cat, you'll get stepped on," she cried out again. Well, that was the end of my patience right there. I, too, started hollering in irritation. Enough is enough, I'm a cat, not a dressing table figurine! The Damsel remained coolly indifferent. She spat out a "Shut up, already, I'm trying to think!" and went back to her work. I was by this stage wildly rattled. What on earth was going on here? According to absolutely credible sources, all writers, great and small, talented and mediocre, have been good friends to us. They were well and truly fond of us. Edgar Allan Poe, Colette, Balzac, Patricia Highsmith, Emmanuel Roides, even the demented Philip K. Dick, they all drew inspiration from us. This is not a figment of my imagination, madam, it is variously recorded that we have always functioned in the role of muse. Could it be that it's all a fib? Or have I crossed paths with an impostor impersonating a writer?

THE CAT WHO TURNED INTO A DOG
WHO TURNED INTO A HUMAN

Naturally, the truth was more complicated. But do let's take things from the start. Antonio Porchia, a friend of mine from the beaux jours of the Great Library, once wrote the following phrase which caused me a great deal of perplexity: *He who can be who he is, is so very little for him who cannot be who he is.* Despite the advantages of the experience of six lives, I could not fully fathom his meaning. On a diet of ocean shrimp, who couldn't be who he is? That is really what it's about, isn't it? Are you kidding us, Mr. Porchia? For eleven years running, I regurgitated it better than if I were a goat but, to be frank, I never did actually get the full meaning. Now, with the wisdom of the seventh life and the sorrow of rejection, I am beginning to understand the dear Antonio: Most creatures on the face of this earth are like Russian dolls; you see one but there's another half dozen lying in wait under the skin.

I will give you an example so you see my point. Mr. Josef, a housemate of mine for four years, in my fourth life, must have been one of those. He was an accomplished carpenter and an excellent family man. At nights, though, he would secretly get up and learn Mandarin through a self-teaching method. When his spouse accidentally found him out, he explained it was because he feared the children's ridicule. What use did a sixty-year-old have for Chinese?

"Actually, what use do you have for it?" his good wife whispered.

"I was thinking of becoming a chef specializing in Chinese cuisine," he whispered back.

"Where? Here?" she went on, askance.

"No, there. In Shanghai, that is."

"Shanghai?" she was flummoxed. "Without asking us? Without consulting with your family?"

"But . . . you aren't my family in that life," he answered after a long pause.

Then, we all thought that he'd gone bonkers, to put it bluntly. Now, I know that, quite simply, he was hiding others in himself, one of whom fancied frying bamboo shoots with rice for a slant-eyed clientele. The human soul is an abyss, in short. But, my dears, so is the feline one, because that very thing happened to me. For better or for worse, it transpired that I had a dog in me who had a human in him!

I had a flash of realization out of the blue, when I remembered the very first phrase I heard come out of her mouth. "I always wanted a dog," she'd said to Mrs. Sweetie. So, that is it. She doesn't let me get in her bed and her books because she doesn't love me. And she doesn't love me because I am not what she wants. By the ocean shrimp, this makes my mission mighty difficult. Not only do I have to teach her to love a cat in his entirety, but in addition, to love a cat even if it's not a dog! Pardon me, dear universe, but not even Jesus from Nazareth had his work cut out in such a manner! I'm sorely tempted to sum things up the same way he did himself: Father, father, why hast thou forsaken me?

The point is that, recalling everything about her behavior, I could suddenly see the whole thing perfectly clearly: She treated me as if I were a dog. She called me and expected me to respond at once, she ordered me and thought it perfectly natural that I obey, she posed as my mistress and considered that I would make do with the role of the underling. Small wonder she hadn't named me Rover, really . . . That is how it is if that is what you think, Damsel. You wish me a dog? I will become one! But promise me that you will allow something of the feline to enter your human dimension as well.

THE CALL OF THE WILD (OR, LOST IN TRANSLATION)

I've heard a great many things in this house. Words sailed above my head night and day: caress-words, bomb-words, slap-words, sleeping-pill-words. Actions hung around in the corners temporarily, waiting for words to give them meaning so they could rise and present themselves. It was there that I realized that the exact same action can be served up by my housemates as an abominable crime or as self-sacrifice, depending on the words chosen to describe it. "Everything is a matter of narrative," the Damsel would say over and over again, in defense of the way she earned a crust. It was confusing, my dears, even for a wise, seventh-life cat. Here is a situation that is indicative of my predicament: Once, when they were having friends over and had served the hors d'oeuvres, I jumped on the table and had a taste of most everything. When she discovered me, she went so red that for a moment I feared that the party would be taking place at the hospital. Now, here are the narrative versions of my action that were voiced on that occasion:

FAVORABLE VERSION (by Christina, a good friend of mine): I feel neglected amidst all the hoopla and need to be made part of the proceedings.

DAMNING VERSION (by the Damsel): I am spoiled and do whatever comes into my head, regardless.

REALISTIC VERSION (mine): I was starving because they'd forgotten to feed me, preoccupied with feeding their friends as they were.

You might wonder whether all this is of any significance. Why, of course it is, you silly coots! If the first version had carried the day, they would pet me apologetically and let me have another treat or two. If the second, I would get smacked with a slipper. And if anyone had eyes for the third, why then, they would serve me my can of food and let me be. In the end, as it happened, none of them did gain currency because the doorbell rang, and the first guests saved me from becoming another cat lost in translation . . .

FREEDOM OR DEATH?

The hardest word, though, by far, was "freedom." What on earth does "freedom" mean? At first, things were fairly simple. Having grown up in a fifth-floor apartment, the word freedom to me meant being able to walk in and out of any room I felt like. So I didn't feel exactly what you'd call free but, as I am not an ingrate, I considered my life fine and dandy. Only I constantly overheard people feeling sorry for me and that started undermining my sense of joy. It was insidious but it was eating away at me. On one occasion, I even got tearful over my case when a friend of the Damsel pensively said, as he stroked me:

"Poor animal, growing up in captivity. It's not his fault. Why should he be leading a life so far removed from nature and from his own true nature? He is neither an animal nor a human being, but rather a hybrid, completely unnatural, condemned to never know the world that he was created to know."

"But . . . ," The Damsel stammered.

"There's no buts," he cut her short. "Can he open the door and just walk out? No! Only when one has the choice to leave but instead stays, only then does one choose freely."

Those words rocked my world, my dears. I got into deep thinking. So, freedom isn't getting inside some place, but, on the contrary, being able to leave? Where I had been looking on myself as a super lucky guy, I suddenly was transformed into someone doing a life sentence. And it all happened by means of a couple of simple sentences! Damned narrative, what traps you set! When the couch philosopher got up to leave, for the first time in my life I ran and sneaked out the door, unobserved by all as they hugged and kissed farewell. The housemates didn't even notice I was missing. They fell straight into bed, as it was five in the morning. I went up two flights of stairs, drunk with freedom, went down three flights appraising freedom as I was becoming familiar with it, went back up two flights, a little worn out by too much freedom at that point and, then, I ended up incredibly bored. The outside world didn't offer much in terms of entertainment value—not to mention it had too many staircases. So I returned to the front door rug and lay there, waiting for the door to open and admit me inside again. Because, my dears, although I've no bone to pick with freedom, I actually like my couch better.

The Damsel located me in the morning after looking everywhere, practically yelling out my name, that's how anxious she got at not seeing me in any of my usual nooks and crannies. She hugged me tightly to herself and smiled. I think she understood immediately what this was about because from then on, every time someone left the house, she let me pretend that I was leaving, only to return of my own will, just before she closed the front door. So we all were happy. I was exercising my free choice and she was alleviated from the stigma of being a prison warden.

But, then, what goes around, comes around, isn't that so? Soon, fate would play a game on me to teach me in the most humiliating manner just what the cost of that notorious freedom is. Summer had arrived again and I was a year and a half old, with my Perfect Whiteness in full bloom. The city was sizzling in the heat wave but I was purring blissfully on the couch, across from the electric fan. You see, I was still at that stage unaware that my housemates had decided, alongside the hoi polloi, to evacuate the city in favor of the nonsensical habit of swimming in the sea. It was the first time they would be leav-

ing our domicile, and my good self with it, for so long a period
and it gave them pause.

"What'll we do with Zach?" Ziggy asked out of the blue.

The Damsel stood stock still, in the middle of packing her
bags. My hairs stood on end. That very question was the beginning, during my second life, of an adventure in which I ended
up in a rubbish dump. I started to shake.

"What do you want us to do with him?" (Yes, what?)

"Who is going to look after him?" (So, that's what you
mean? Phew! I was worried there for a bit . . .)

"Christina." (The person answering to this name had started
out as the Damsel's sister and gradually ended up as mine. For
details, see the chapter below, "The feline-ness of strangers.")

"But we'll be gone a month." (Whaaat? A month?)

"So?" (Jeez, have a heart, you callous goon!)

"He'll freak out in here all by himself." (Quite so!)

"I don't think so. He'll be fine." (Oh, no, he won't, callous
goon!)

"Maybe we should take him over to my mother's?"
(Aaaargh!)

" . . . " (Don't, please, consider it, Damsel. Say no! Say no!)

"He'll have a ball at my mother's, I'm sure of it." (You,
dearie, can go jump off a cliff, and take your certainty with
you.)

"You think?" (I can't believe this! She's buying it.)

At this point I jump off the couch and ostentatiously absent
myself, to indicate my disagreement.

"Yeah, sure. Why should the poor guy stay by himself all
these weeks? There's a yard there, too. The poor kitty can
enjoy a bit of freedom for a change!" (Oh oh, I can just see
myself going up and down stairs all over again.)

"Hmmm . . . alright. Fine. Let's take him there." (Hey, don't
I get a say in this?)

I, my friends, was left speechless. These humans, who supposedly loved me, were deciding on my behalf without so much as taking the trouble to find out where I stood on the matter. *Inconceivable!* It made no difference, my nervous coming and going through all the rooms like crazy, no difference that a whole international bibliography was emphatic about cats *detesting* moving, that I hid under couches or that I scooped out the dirt from every single flowerpot in the balcony; they were under the impression that I was insanely happy about my transfer to Mrs. Sweetie's yard. And you know why? Because that's what suited them. In order for their conscience not to be burdened with the thought of doing me harm (abandoning me) they did me a greater one (moving me). I got the rough end of the deal just like the old lady the boy scout drags across the street against her will, so he can tick off his good deed for the day. As I think it over, I'm surprised as to why it made such an impression on me back then. It's something humans do all the time. Haven't you seen them willy nilly carrying their aged parents from their beautiful villages to the horrible cities? If you ask them why, they hypocritically answer, "So the poor souls aren't on their own." In truth, they leave them even more alone in filthy one-room basements or old-age pensions, depriving them of their village home, their friend the coffee shop owner, and their pal the goat. By the ocean shrimp, they are the greatest hypocrites!

So they shoved me in my carry basket and took me straight to Mrs. Sweetie's place. It even occurred to them to stay for dinner, supposedly so they could check how easily I would adjust to the new environment. (Unmerciful translation: because they coveted Mr. Jean's pork ribs.) During the trip I kept meowing forlornly. I felt sorry I didn't have a flag I could fly at half-mast over my carry basket. When we finally arrived, they opened it in the middle of the garden and let me out. The Damsel, meanwhile, had started getting suspicious. "You wait and see: He'll freak out once we leave," she whispered. Ziggy and Mrs.

Sweetie on the other hand, thought otherwise. They pointed to the spot I had left so I wouldn't have to look at their mugs and they exclaimed: "Nah, not a chance! Just look at him. He found a garden and he is overjoyed. He's relishing his freedom. He doesn't give two hoots about you!" (Congrats all round. You obviously possess the hereditary gift of thought reading!)

So they steadfastly ignored me and then left, after each had about thirty pork ribs apiece. Night had come. Strange noises started from behind the bushes. Well, Madam Sweetie, let me draw a line right here; as deeply as I cherish my freedom, there's no way I'm spending the night in this jungle. So I quickly sneaked inside through the open kitchen door and hid under the couch. Next morning, as a result of all the distress, I had a fever. Clearly, I looked like death because Sweetie got the message straight away, took me to a decent doctor and started me on antibiotics. Let it be noted that my hypocrite housemates called from time to time, because they were supposedly worried about my health. Nonsense, my dears. Just keeping up appearances.

Two weeks went by and the truth is I had adjusted well, whether willingly or not. I had even started getting bold and leaving the kitchen for short strolls in the grass, always under the supervision of Sweetie. This freedom business wasn't half bad, after all. As soon, though, as I felt completely safe and master of the situation, I made the fatal mistake. I heard through the adjacent fence the sounds of a group of cats partying and having a grand old time. Listening to all that meowing here, there and everywhere, the beast woke up in me. I am a cat, too, and I was tempted to do a bit of courting myself. In the fifth floor where those two held me captive (yes, that's right, I had now woken to the fact of my captivity) the only female I had available was the red leather armchair, which is why I had clawed it to bits. So I ostentatiously left the veranda where Sweetie and Jean were having their coffee and—to their great surprise—I entered full of confidence and with much posing in the yard next door to choose the dark object of my desire. A mistake of the greatest order, my dears! Before I'd had a chance to check things out, three wild commando-cats were onto me, extremely irritated that I had turned up uninvited on their little turf. In two nanoseconds flat, my Perfect Whiteness was bleeding. My heart sped up to advanced aerobic rate and I—don't ask me how—ejected myself as if I had turbine propellers in my butt, leapt over the fence in cartoon-like fashion and landed by Sweetie's feet, terrified out of my wits. This is no exaggeration, unfortunately. I had literally shat myself! Sweetie still laughs when she recounts my misadventure, which she always finishes by saying: "Ah, Zach dear, set a beggar on a horse and he'll ride to the devil!" Well, ma'am, I didn't happen to know that freedom has such sharp nails and I was duly punished for it. But you ought to know that you must spare the dishonored from further maligning. The punishment for your ignorance will be the two days you'll have to spend restoring my ass to its former pristine condition!

Of course, there's no bad without some good. Out of this mishap I derived two precious conclusions:

a) Don't listen to the nincompoops who pity you for your life of captivity. When it comes down to it, we all live inside some kind of wall. It's just that some fail to see the fence of their own enclosure due to spiritual myopia.

b) In defeat, you can actually score great victories! My humiliating adventure, paradoxically, moved the Damsel greatly. Without realizing it, she had Anna, the heroine of her novel, humiliate herself in the erotic arena because she simply didn't meet the requirements for winning. Characteristically, the title of the chapter in question was the refrain of my own little drama: Put a beggar on a horse . . . (Zach, my boy, I can't say if you are free or not, but you most certainly are a living inspiration!)

How I got in her bed
(and back out straight away)

The Damsel had a soft spot for her bed. I could tell at first glance. In her own words, "All the nice things take place there: rest, sleep, contemplation, sex, reading, eating." What she meant was that *she* did all those things there. It took ages before I finally understood that she also devised the plots of her novels there, in perfect complicity with her unconscious—I don't know if you follow, as, at first, I myself couldn't.

The extremely few times I managed to sneak unobserved into her bedroom, I saw her open her eyes but not get up. She would sit there for an hour like a zombie, neither asleep nor quite awake. In the twilight zone. Every so often she'd leap up, grab a pen and scribble wherever she could reach—usually in the back, blank pages of books—and then go back into the aforementioned coma. By the ocean shrimp, I couldn't figure it out. What was she scribbling, if she was napping? And why spoil perfectly good books and not grab one of the countless notepads strewn everywhere in the house?

Months later, I heard her explain to a friend of hers. As soon as you open your eyes, she said, just at the moment when you cross the threshold of the unconscious (sleep) to enter consciousness (being awake) your brain operates at the Alpha level. Don't ask what the hell that Alpha level is, I'm not that sure myself. At all events, that is where all the treasures are supposedly piled that we have gathered in our lives: experiences, thoughts, fantasies, desires, sounds, fears, information, impressions. Something like a dream storehouse. In that buried treasury, the Damsel extends the hand of consciousness and collects her material. And now you know as much as I do. What is for certain is: a) this is where I urgently needed to sneak into, so she'd fish me out as well; and, b) she is an incorrigible slob who systematically destroys her books because she never takes care to have a notepad by her side.

In addition to fishing for ideas in the bedroom, The Damsel sleeps. She sleeps a lot. Why humans charge us cats with being sleepyheads, when they lay themselves down and can't be budged with a crane before eight hours have been and gone, is beyond me. We cats do take our naps at regular intervals but we are also on the alert. I also find it rather rude, my dears. If you choose to sleep till you rot, so to speak, well then, you can't just shut me out on my own for all those hours. Let me in and then you can lay there forever and a day!

The truth is that I do have a small share of responsibility for my exile from her haven. The very first time I managed to get inside—after many hours of siege during which my meowing and sniveling reduced her to a nervous wreck—I was a tiny bit greedy and inconsiderate. At first, I clambered onto the southernmost part of the bed, where her feet normally rest. With bogus restraint, I took up a little corner on the bedcovers and I waited. As soon as I was sure she wasn't responding, I moved into stage two of my siege: I sneakily crawled under the eiderdown. Again no response. Perfect! Evidently, drowsiness had lowered her resistance and the citadel was mine for the taking! I started inching my way upwards. "Hey, you, where do you think you're going?" her voice was heard in the dark. "Let him in, he's cold," Ziggy said. (For some inexplicable reason, men were always kinder to me. As you'll see, they empathized, protected me, fed me and put up with me with a smile on their face. Unfortunately, however, my target was this incorrigible woman.) She let me be for a bit. Well, this was the point at

which I went too far; instead of sitting tight, I climbed even higher with the end result that my hefty tail ended up across her face. The Damsel leapt up as if she'd been stepped on by an elephant, yelling, "I swear, this cat is as bad as my ex, you give him an inch and he wants a mile!" Needless to say I ended up spending the night outside their bed. Likewise, it goes without saying that she replaced the handle on the bedroom door with one so heavy not even a bear could dislodge it.

The most interesting thing, though, was that the next morning when the Damsel was fishing for ideas in the Alpha level, the phrase that kept surfacing was "He's just like my ex." A cat like a human. The next association was *The Planet of the Apes*, a film where apes are like humans and humans are like apes. Well, after that, reversals of all kinds started occurring to her at lightning speed. And, reversal upon reversal, the Damsel's mind fished up her next book, where boys behave like girls and girls behave like boys! (Zach, my boy, you are evolving into a mega-muse!)

THE WINTER OF OUR DISCONTENT

Time went by and a year arrived so strange that its summer looked worryingly like wintertime. The housemates were as usual making ready to leave, and go write on an island somewhere. But nothing was normal. I felt this even if I couldn't understand it, and it was getting on my nerves. I don't mean the nerves I got into as soon as I saw suitcases getting lugged down from the loft. This time it was different. I was finding fault with everything. I was scratching the walls purposelessly. I haunted one room after the next like a ghost, didn't eat, didn't drink and was constantly chasing my tail like an imbecile. But they were in a similarly sorry state themselves. They barely spoke, whereas normally they had volumes to say (and now I understand why: the things you cannot speak about, you must pass over in silence); they were given to small nervous gestures, they banged the doors without realizing it . . . It was a very weird thing, like war disguised as peace.

The icing on the cake came on the day before departure; Ziggy again proposed the inimitable idea of moving me to Sweetie's for the whole of August! I was outraged. I wove in and out of the Damsel's legs meowing beseechingly, on the off chance she might extend me some protection. But her mind was elsewhere, my anxiety was the least of her concerns. So, for the second time, I found myself in the familiar carry basket in the familiar car, that deposited me in the familiar house of Sweetie in a state of acute mourning. This time, however, they didn't spend any time monitoring my adjustment. They got back in their car and they disappeared from the face of the earth.

That August was as dark as December. I was floundering in bad feelings. Our forefathers of old were known for their prophetic insight, which is why humans worshipped them as deities—and then burned them in pyres alongside witches. (Because that is how humans are in the face of remarkable creatures, my dears. Undecided about whether to hate them or worship them. Meow No. 984.) I personally only once delivered an unforgettable prophecy, in which I predicted a disaster. It was a September night, in 1999, when I felt danger approach. The housemates had retired to their chambers (with the door shut, of course) and I was looking for a way to notify them. Thus, I initiated a nocturnal concert of disturbances: Howling, door scratching, thumps and thuds, I used everything at my disposal. After much ado and once they'd made up their minds that I wasn't going to allow them to lie peacefully in the arms of Morpheus, the Damsel got up, came into the living room and picked me up in her arms, in the hope that this might shut me up. I, however, was determined to keep up the racket until she realized that I wasn't being perverse, I was a bearer of ill omens. Finally, I concentrated and, with a leap, I got into the Damsel's mind, which was no mean feat. I made it because: a) she kept looking into my eyes trying to figure out what was wrong with me; and, b) our bodies were in close contact. I knew it had happened because she immediately stood up and said to herself, "Hey, you don't say, there might be an earthquake?" Then she ran to her desk and saved a disc copy of the book she was writing at the time. After she had the copy safely in her bag, she lay on the couch and we slept in each other's arms.

The next day she was recounting my behavior to a group of friends at her office. The foolish folk were hooting with laughter as she held up the disc when, lo and behold, the building started shaking and books started to rain down from the bookshelves. "Zach was right!" one of the girlfriends exclaimed. "Not even a seismologist could make such a prediction!" The outcome was twofold; the circle of friends started calling me by the surname of one of the celebrated seismologists of the day and they pleaded with the Damsel to let them know in case of a repeat demonstration of my oracular powers!

The next earthquake, unfortunately, was in my lifestyle. I was on Sweetie's kitchen floor trying to fathom the origin of my feelings of foreboding when I heard, to my horror, that I would be migrating for a second time that week. Jean wanted us all to go to his village! I shall be brief. I went catatonic until we arrived. The village turned out to be terminally rustic. All in all, five houses, all in bad taste, inhabited by sixteen individuals with bad taste. I was abandoned in the yard. In villages rife with poor taste, as is common knowledge, cats avoid houses that evidence poor taste and busy themselves hunting mice and snakes. In short, my dears, I was forced to abide by the ancient customs of the countryside just like my not so very ancient forefathers. I took up a corner and was masochistically chewing my fur which, in any event, was severely affected by summer molting. I knew from experience (cf. chapter on riding beggars) that any moment now, the local village cats would turn up to make mincemeat of me.

Well and truly, within half an hour on the outside, they ferreted me out from the corner of the shed where I had slunk, and tore me to shreds as if I were a red armchair. My heavenward cries *at last* alerted Madam Sweetie who came outside and collected me. The doctor diagnosed a large puncture on my left foot, disinfected it, sprayed it with liquid gauze, and ordered them to look out for me. Now, madam, is that something you need the doctor to tell you? How can you abandon such a high-class cat (or such a wuss, whatever) in that stable? Don't you see all the cats in the area look like Rambo, only worse off for all the mauling?

After all that, I spent my time in a corner, attracting as little attention as possible, until I had healed. I was counting the days. I was naïve enough to believe that the end of August would spell the end of my trials. Naturally, that isn't how things turned out. (Naturally, things hardly ever turn out the way we expect. Naturally, we pick quarrels with the things that will not bend to our will. And, naturally, things continue as they will, notoriously indifferent to our wants and wishes. I don't know why I am going on about it, it just never fails to make an impression.) Anyway, when the housemates turned up to pick me up from Sweetie, I got scared. Yes, alright, the atmosphere had been somewhat tense before. Only now it was funereal. How on earth did such a thing happen? What killed off my favorite duet? Why did they ever suddenly start performing solo, and so pitifully? (Because everything is in flow, Heraclitus would answer. Because the universe is expanding, Woody Allen would answer. Just because, the ignorant hoi polloi would answer.)

In the days that followed, our warm little home turned into Alaska, my dears. They had each occupied a wing—the Damsel to the east of her office, Ziggy to the west of the living room. The empty bedroom in the middle, a neutral zone. I was sure they had come to some kind of agreement and were stoically counting days before breaking up for good. I didn't know exactly what that deal might be, nor why they went about as silently as ghosts. Not a sound, my dears. I'd never found myself in a worse position. First of all, I was accustomed to a diet of hugs and kisses, naturally. I'd much rather they hurl slippers and swear at me for leaving hairs everywhere, anything but this creepy silence. The fact that I did look a fair bit like an Eskimo notwithstanding, Alaska, to me, was a hostile, unfamiliar country. I couldn't take it. By the ocean shrimp, I wished with all my heart I was the Cheshire Cat who disappeared whenever he fancied, leaving behind only a smile. I was getting dizzy from all the pressure. I was coming and going ceaselessly between the two camps like a United Nations blue beret, in a state of extreme anxiety, trying my best to come up with a solution. Some idea that would open up their hearts and mouths. Something to glue back together the broken pieces. I've said it before, my dears, and I'll say it again: Cats can't stand changes. If we lose someone important, we are likely to sicken and die ourselves. What did I just say? Sicken? *Eureka!* Well done, my boy. You are to get urgently and critically sick. I've read my share of novels, I know what I'm talking about. Death doth not part, it unites.

The "moribund project" went into immediate effect and was diabolically simple. I sat ostentatiously in the neutral zone and started being sorrowful. I slowly let the world go heavy inside of me. Despair, as you know, only requires the slightest opening to infiltrate your entire space in no time, like the tide. I'd read some findings in my sixth life proving that our immune system's T-cells are literally decimated by despair and that's how we get sick. (Come on, then, sorrow, do your thing and turn me into a quivering mess because I'm telling you, I can't handle it anymore!)

And so it happened. Within two days, the wound in my left foot became infected and a pustule was growing invisibly on the inside. OMG, I am a living metaphor, I thought. Something was secretly rotting away in our kingdom and now it would manifest on me. I am the screen on which their drama will be projected. Indeed, on the morning of the third day, as the Damsel was stroking me, she passed her hand over the afflicted area. The allegedly healed wound opened and copious quantities of pus started to run out. The Damsel, who was receptive to living metaphors, got the message straight away and started to cry—supposedly for me. (This business with you humans is starting to get on my nerves. Why can't you for once directly and honestly admit what is happening inside of you?

Why, for instance, do you always say that you are not divorcing for the sake of the kids? Whom are you kidding? The plain truth is that you are scared witless to make the change; which, from experience, I do have a certain amount of sympathy with.)

So I made it. Out of necessity, the silence was lifted. The Damsel ran over to the Western Zone and announced to Ziggy that Zach (I) was very sick. She was talking to him and the tears were streaming down her face. Suddenly they were an item again. They leafed through agendas, made desperate phone calls, turned the world upside down and came up with one clinic that was open at night, somewhere near the northern suburbs. The put me in the car and drove me over, silent again. Once we arrived, I was hurriedly ushered into surgery and they were left waiting. When I got out I was wearing a despicable Elizabethan collar meant to stop me from messing with my wound. My wound is internal, you idiots, I felt like screaming at the doctors. And there's no collar that can stop me messing with it.

As they were driving me back to the house, I was peeking desperately behind the damned collar trying to figure out if my trick had worked. It hadn't. The Alaskan cold froze up every word before it came out of their mouths. You failed, my boy, I told myself. They had been one, but were back to being two again. The law of entropy had claimed us.

That night I didn't sleep. I knew the time I feared had come: the time to say the great yes or the great no. After banging for hours with my collar against all the doors and walls of the house, I collapsed in the neutral zone in a heap. Why were they doing this to me? Whom would I choose now? Who would I part with? I would have a better life with him. He always paid more attention to me, he loved me and he accepted me. My meals came at the proper time, my litter was cleaned out with the greatest punctuality. He was a regular daddy. He fully took

me on under his care with no complaint, although he saw me
begging for her company. She, on the contrary, wasn't willing
to shoulder any responsibility. The slightest grumpiness on my
part annoyed her. She called me "double trouble." It was
inconceivable to her that I should demand anything. She saw
me as a kind of pal that she had accepted to put up for a while.
"Relax, buddy, and make do as best you can," she told me once
when I was complaining because she served me plain milk,
having forgotten to get me a can. And then she ended up with
the same offensive refrain: "Don't be a glutton, fatso!" (I'm
not being a glutton, ma'am. Did you ever try to fill up on plain
milk?)

Anyway, I knew the score. It would be rough but it was with
her I had to go. First of all, to teach her to love a being from
head to paw, all of it. Secondly, so that I could grow up as well.
People who understand their cats too well, keep them at an
infantile level. Do you want some treats, my Zach? There you
go! Do you want some cuddling? There you go! But when the
Damsel said, "There you go!" she usually meant "get thee gone
from my sight." That hurt my feelings but it kept me in fighting
form. Besides, there were the literary considerations: I'd gone
through so much trouble to start getting into her books, I would
hate to see it wasted. So, it was decided—she was my karma.

A little before dawn I went to check up on him. He was
sleeping, curled up on the sofa. I said goodbye inwardly, sending him a trillion love molecules, and went over to her office
where she was temporarily spending the nights, in a sleeping
bag. The doors weren't closed anymore—the divide that had
gone up between the office and the living room was so impenetrable that doors were redundant. I crawled butt first into the
sleeping bag and tried to make myself comfortable. Without
properly waking up she said, "It's you, fatso?" and moved over
a bit to make some space for me. I never slept better. I was sad
but calm. I had made my choice.

In the morning I woke her up by massaging her neck. She opened her eyes with difficulty. "Morning, baby bear," she said and kissed my ear. The book she started to write straight after that was called *In the Singular*. The main character, named Aris, was a real sweetheart and his friend Hera always called him "fatso" and "baby bear." Now, does that remind you of anything?

HER EGO AND ME

This was the beginning of the new era. I must confess that the Damsel proved a natural when it came to new beginnings—it was with denouements that she was at a loose end. They quite plainly didn't suit her, they paralyzed her, cancelled her out. She therefore tended to constantly accelerate them. Let a soul whose time has come, go, she used to say. We will stand and take the blow but no need to drag on the tear 'n' wear, the ambivalence, the misery. Let's move forward, already.

The truth be known, I, too, disdained the fallen who will not get up so as not to risk falling again. Still, I thought there was something suspect about her preoccupation with new beginnings, her impatience to build up from the ground something sparklingly new, unblemished and perfect, untouched by decay, something bearing the promise of all good things. What is life, madam? Do you perchance think it's a Hollywood movie where you can edit out the scenes that get the public down? Say you do move on, what do you expect you'll come across? Your familiar self smiling sardonically, that's what. Anyway. I didn't oppose her. It wasn't the time. We were getting ready to live through a difficult but interesting phase. Besides, we are all a little bit boring at our happiest. Like advertisements of ourselves.

The first thing the Damsel did with the dawn of the first day of the new era was buy paints and rollers and start maniacally painting the house. As I watched her feverishly coat with color every available surface, I got disquieted. What would Ziggy say if he could see her? That guy had fought long and hard to restrain her unbridled worship of Technicolor. And behold, he'd barely turned the corner and the faucets of color were turned on to the max. The house was flooded. (I know that when the cat's away, the mice will play, but beware, Damsel, the cat is still here.) Eventually, her office turned out peach-pink, the bedroom deep green with red poppies, evidently symbolizing the spring that was so keenly anticipated in the middle of autumn, the hall was turquoise, the house heaters red, green and violet, the living room table pale blue, the chairs, dead red. Shall I go on? By the end of the day it looked as if a rainbow had exploded inside our house!

That, naturally, wasn't the only thing that changed. Everything was stood on its head from the moment we became two. The item is now made up of us two, was the first thing I thought, feeling moved. We'll be as tight as the shoe and the sock. Now, I have more rights—and more obligations, too, of course. I urgently need to become less of a cat. I need to let the dog in me out so that she'll love me like I was human.

There was, nevertheless, a tiny bit of an issue. In all honesty and though it's not in my favor, I have to say, my dears, that in general, I was contemptuous of dogs. I'm no speciesist, but let's be frank, they simply don't have our classiness. First of all, they constantly want your attention, they demand long walks twice daily or they bring the house down with barking or they crap in the middle of the living room and, worst of all, with this tendency of theirs to want to be as thick as thieves, they show no respect for anybody's private space. (By the ocean shrimp! While writing this, I'm getting increasingly worried. All this does ring a bell somehow. But it's impossible to figure out what about . . .) The thing, though, that always annoyed me was the brainwashing the average human has been sub-jected to in favor of dogs and, consequently, against us cats.

Because the average human in question is hopelessly insecure and flattered by the pathetic doggedness (if you'll allow the term) of dogs, our autonomy has been misconstrued as insensitivity. Thousands of stories have sung the praises of (i.e. advertised) the dog's loyalty to its (sic) master. How many of you, however, know of the proverbial devotion of the giant white cat of Koumoundouros (Greek nineteenth century politician for those wondering—there's a square named after him, already!), who not only never left his friend's side while he was breathing his last, but himself retired and died immediately afterwards? His pack of dogs, on the contrary, went on with business as usual and as for his political allies, they did a bold turnabout and joined the ranks of his opponent Trikoupis. This is the basic truth, my dears—and do, please, spare me the postmodernist crap about the subjective perception of historical reality.

I, in any event, put all selfishness aside and did my bit as a proper partner. I made sure I followed her everywhere so she could find me there as soon as she needed me. I was under the impression that my intentions were perfectly transparent. I am your knight, Damsel, I would say, swishing my tail, you can count on me. Unfortunately she proved unteachable. She kept looking at me puzzled and every so often she got exasperated and wondered out loud, "Zach, why are you following me around all the time? Have you lost your marbles?"

I didn't give up, of that you can be sure. I persisted. I stalked. The most appropriate time was usually in the dark of night, when there weren't any "guests," as she used to lie on the couch to watch a series she downloaded from the Internet. Then, when she was more susceptible, so to speak, I would gradually start putting my plan into action. First I jumped on the couch next to her, then inched closer till we were touching, then, if she let me, I would climb into her arms. The greatest obstacle in my mission, I must note, was her clothes. The more color the Damsel offloaded onto the furniture and walls, the more she subtracted from her wardrobe. It was like a throng of black crows was nesting in her closet: black skirts, black dresses, black coats, black bags . . . She had the dress sense of an existentialist widow. Lord have mercy! You might think that it was handy, her being all black, me being all white, a fetching combination, right? Not so! I molted terribly you see, against the black background, to the point where she was beside herself with exasperation. She would throw me off her as if I were a leech sucking up her lifeblood, yelling, "Oh, no, not again, Zach, you made a right mess of me again, I can't take this anymore, now how am I to go out with your dirty hairs all over me?" (How can you use that tone of voice with me, madam? You forget that I am the cat of divorced parents?)

As you realize, the first roadblock I had to skirt was the wardrobe. If the clothes weren't black, if they weren't freshly laundered, if they weren't overly delicate, if they weren't her favorite, then she would let me snuggle in her arms. Once there, I lay low and quietly waited for a scene with suspense, at which point I took the opportunity of strategically placing myself under her hand, so she would stroke me. Have you not even a shred of dignity, you might ask. No respect for your Perfect Whiteness? Well, the answer is negative, my dears. I really do think dignity is overrated. I was determined to do whatever it took, to get the love I deserved. If she were ice, I would light a fire to melt her. If she were a rock, I would turn into a wave to erode her. If she forgot to reach her hand out and stroke me, I put my head under her hand so she'd be embarrassed at allowing me to embarrass myself to get one small caress. If I were Leonard Cohen, I would sing *I'm Your Cat* to her. In short, I would do anything that was necessary to teach her love, which, as has been aptly put, endures everything and so on and so forth.

And I was indeed gaining ground. Not a whole lot, a mere

inch at a time. Mostly, it was enough for me. That's something, I could console myself. Gradually, the citadel will fall. Except sometimes I got disheartened. Especially when we had visitors around, I would start feeling low. Don't misunderstand me, I was sociable to a fault. It's common knowledge that cats don't normally trust new people. As soon as a stranger comes into the house, they are alarmed. They run and hide under beds and sofas. I, on the other hand, was the exact opposite. The minute anyone was through the door, I went all out to welcome them, sniff them, roll over for them and generally be as winsome as I knew how to. I did love them all and they loved me back. ("Just look at our Zach the Socialite, turning it on again," the Damsel would say, laughing.) I even assaulted with friendly intent a crew from the electricity company who were over to fix some wiring. I was at my happiest going from one pair of arms to the next all night long, like a courtesan. But when she tried to get a show out of me against my will, I was livid. It is next to unthinkable, what hoops she made me jump through. She would drag me on the ground by my front legs calling, "There's my good fatso, there's my Zach the Mop, plenty of dust around here for you to be useful." I obliged her. She grabbed me by the legs and rotated me as if I were a Ferris wheel. I put up with it. Then she would hurl me up to a height for the spectacle-loving audience to admire my dexterity in landing on all fours. It's true we have a knack for doing that. Even if you drop us from the fourth floor, we are flexible enough to set ourselves right so as to land on our paws, whose thickness absorbs the impact. You would break every bone in your body, but not us. What of it, though? Was it right for her to set me up as the party clown and acrobat so she could get a laugh out of her guests? Still, what was I to do? I suffered everything with a happy face. (Love endures everything and so on.)

The worst though, the one that hurt my feelings, was when

she made me do the trick of stealing a caress for her friends to marvel at my stealth and slyness. "Come, my Zach, there, see, I'm just letting my hand dangle, come and stick your head underneath and get it stroked." I know what you're going to say. Why did I do it? Why didn't I walk off to make a point, to insult her in front of everyone? The answer, my dears, is simple. Life is too short. (Meow No. 777: You mustn't let any opportunity to be stroked go to waste. It's a sinful waste to die unstroked.)

Now that I see it all from a distance, I can put it into words: She was so absorbed in her readings, her writings, her friends, her hatreds and her passions—her ego in short—that it was as if I didn't count. She was terribly bothered by my hairs everywhere. No matter how I tried to camouflage them, they were white and long; you couldn't miss them from a mile away. Especially every spring and at the beginning of summer, in her irritation, she used to call me "the meandering hair loss." She also took objection to my habit of chewing up the flowers she was sent by her various and sundry love interests. Yet I found those flowers annoying. I knew how things went—first the bouquet appears, then its enamored sender. No, thank you, I will not allow any such liberties to be taken on my home ground.

Anything I did, really, seemed to her strange—as in weird. And I really need to ask, my dears. Hundreds of books had been through her hands, why did she never take the trouble to read a manual of practical cat rearing so she could get her bearings? Why did she come after me, hurling slippers every time I scratched my nails on some surface? What did she expect me to do? Like our forefathers of old, we, too, need to trim and sharpen our claws by dragging them across a hard surface. Rather than wielding rifles and bazookas, Damsel, we have these as our armaments. I looked for hard surfaces in the house and found them on the living room table, the kitchen chairs and the sofa on the veranda. Those were what I came across, so those were what I used for my necessary pedicure. The red leather armchair wasn't a hard surface as such but it was so pretty that I ripped it to shreds to see what was further inside. (How right they are when they say curiosity killed the cat! The Damsel, who was very partial to her chair, gave me chase with a hiking boot in her hand, outraged. Do you have any idea what those boots weigh? Three kilograms apiece! I spent a week on alert under the bookshelf in the hall.)

On a different occasion, she came back home tired and found me in an admittedly original situation. I was in the middle of the living room floor which was bespattered with blood and feathers. There was blood on my fur, too, especially around the mouth and paws—Count Dracula in the flesh. The Damsel was flabbergasted. "What happened, Zach my darling?" she inquired with a tender concern never shown before. She must have thought I was the victim, you see, of some terrible attack. As soon, however, as she glimpsed the corpse of the unfortunate pigeon I had (almost) devoured, she went bonkers. She took to cleaning up the blood and feathers while simultaneously castigating me as if I were a freak of nature. She called me a vampire, a bloodthirsty monster, an incubus. For my part, I felt bad on the one hand and puzzled on the other. Had she completely forgotten I was a carnivore? Pigeons are our pork ribs, Damsel, it's natural for us to hunt them. How would you like it if I called you a bloodthirsty monster next time you ordered a hamburger with large fries and extra mustard?

Her worst time by far was when I sprayed around the house as a way of pointing out that my time had come for a bit of sex. A point of clarification: I am deeply grateful, Damsel, that you didn't hasten to turn me into a eunuch, only there are consequences, as you might well have been apprised, had you taken an interest. The effects of my incarceration in your penthouse monastery may have been decisive, I may well have lost my zing and my kinkiness, but I wasn't entirely out of commission yet! Since there was no available female inside, I sprayed the sexy red armchair (the ripped one), the worn postman's leather bag with her smell on it and the kitchen table which smelled of pork chops. I, too, had my rights in life, in love and inside this house, and seeing she wasn't paying notice, my stink was my way of letting her know. "Get up, stand up, stand up for your rights," as Bob Marley has it.

All of that, of course, was the exception rather than the rule. Basically, I was asexual. Once only, I recall, I saw from a distance a beautiful kindred Persian and felt a piercing stab in my heart. I was on the fifth-floor balcony and she was proudly walking in the street, unaware of my very existence. I silently whispered to her the verse of Baudelaire and let her walk out of my life forever:

A lightning flash . . . then night! Fleeting beauty
By whose glance I was suddenly reborn
Will I see you no more before eternity?

Damn it, here I go, getting all soppy. Isn't there a soul to pass me a fried shrimp to make things alright?

LONELY PLANET

Yet nothing cast a shadow on our relationship more than her travels. I don't mean to play innocent. As the Damsel said over and over again in her discussions with her friends that went on till dawn, you can know everything about a person within the first hour of meeting them—provided you want to. I can only second that. Even a blind man could have seen that first day on the lawn that she was incapable of staying put—she was coming and going like a spinning top, asking questions, looking around, wanting to have a poke at everything, including the nest of my misanthropic mother. I knew who I was heading for and, as I hope you recall, I went straight to her. I was asking for it, as the saying goes.

It was equally evident that: a) she wasn't pining for company (the furry, four-legged variety, that is; she was fine with the two-legged kind); and, b) she was not willing to take on responsibilities. I went and adopted her despite all that, brave as a Greek and determined to fulfill my mission. Still, all things have a limit, my dears. How the devil am I to fulfill the mission of training someone when that someone is away all the time? Via teleconference? I'm a cat, not a lecturer at Open University. In addition, how on earth am I supposed to spend my entire time just playing with my tail and tearing up the (already shredded) red armchair?

In actual fact, that issue came up at the same time as the color explosion in our home. As long as we lived with Ziggy, a sworn cat lover, everything that concerned my good self was going just fine. Ziggy grounded her. He would stand up to her. He kept her travels in check. As soon, however, as my personal benefactor packed his suitcase and left the house, she also packed hers and was scarcely to be seen ever since! Alright, I'm exaggerating, I did see her, though only for as long as it took her to organize the next trip. She behaved like a kid whose parents are away, drunk on the sudden freedom.

First off, there were the professional trips. In addition to being a writer she was a historian, and needed to attend historical conferences—fine, I got that. Work is work, and there were bills to pay. My tin food was strictly gourmet and on the pricy side. (Sorry kiddos in Africa but, seriously, does anyone believe that if I starve, all of a sudden there will be paella raining down from the sky on your village?) Apart, however, from being a historian, she was a writer, which meant, she said, that she had to travel to her book presentations in case some overseas agent got interested enough to launch her international career. (Ha!) Being generous at heart, I filed this, too, in a work context—although what actually took place was somewhat different: The touring Greek writers ate and drank at the alehouses of Frankfurt and the bars of Berlin, while the potential customers were being courteously indifferent.

The worst of all, however, the most needless and—alas!— the longest in duration, were the mountaineering trips. I'm no dark, brooding type, but I confess I loathed with every fiber of my being those enthusiasts who abandoned their loved ones on festive days, in order to go climb the world's mountains and outcrops, for no good reason. They rushed like lunatics to the most improbable spots on the planet just so they could have a rough time. Vietnam, New Zealand, Ethiopia, Venezuela are but a few I could mention. By the ocean shrimp, I felt like keeling over and dying every time I saw the hated red backpack coming down from the loft along with the batons, the fleece outfit and the rainproof but breathable Gore-Tex membranes. I used to climb on the pack at night and chew the braces that kept the water canteen attached. Once I peed inside the sleeping bag. It was all in vain. Nothing ever stopped her.

The one occasion when I wouldn't dream of whining was whenever I heard she was off to Berlin. First of all, that was the home city of my good pal Zach H(uman). He was a sweetheart like me, smart as anything, like me, a fan of Emmanuel Roides like me, adorable like me, wise like me and last but not least, a Zach like me! Unfortunately we never did meet—he never travelled to Athens, I never travelled to Berlin (or anywhere else for that matter); it was one of those modern, long distance relationships. Besides, according to Zach H., you didn't need to be thick as thieves in order to prove your love. All the same, we did see each other on a daily basis: he had put up a most photogenic portrait of me in the collection of his friends' pictures in his kitchen and I spent hours contemplating his photograph which the Damsel had on the second shelf in her library. Most importantly, he always asked after me, laughed at my heroics and excused my antics. So, it made good sense to consent to her visits to him.

To be sure, there was one trip to Berlin which I never did forgive her. A few days before her scheduled flight, she had become involved in a fiery affair with Beefcake. On the outside, Beefcake seemed to have it all: he was kind, he was tall, he was handsome, he was talented. Still, as it turned out, he was a bit short in self-confidence. The day the Damsel was due to leave he had an attack of insecurity. I could tell that he was suddenly not too sure about where things between them were heading. Did they have a relationship or didn't they? Could it all have been a momentary lapse? So, in the blink of an eye, he decided to take me hostage to make sure that the Damsel would have to go and see him on her return. (The joke was that a blind man could see the Damsel was dying to have something long-term with him. But, this is a point I have made repeatedly: My dears, you are deafer than the deaf and blinder than the blind.

The only one who took stock of his dark scheme was me. The Damsel was far too busy admiring his chiseled torso. The truth is I did have a sort of a gift—the Damsel used to mock me, saying I had scanners for eyes. My scanners, then, started sounding the alarm when I heard the first—seemingly innocent—line:

He: "You are leaving tomorrow morning?" (In a horrified tone.) "And where will you leave your charge?" (In a tone that affected interest.) You mustn't hasten to think me prejudiced: That man had been in our house for twenty-four hours and hadn't once reached down to pet me!

The Damsel smiled at him tenderly. She thought he had a bleeding heart for me. She was that far gone.

SHE: "Right here. Zach is fine with that." (Madam, it is you who says so, nobody else.)

HE: "You mean to say you just drop him like that, the poor thing, and disappear for a week?" (As you surmise, intelligent readers, Beefcake is referring to himself. For my good self, he couldn't care less.)

SHE: "Oh, come now. It's no big deal. I go away all the time. Zach is perfectly used to it." (Again, madam, it is only you who says so.)

HE: "And who is going to feed him?" (What do you care, pal?)

SHE: "Christina." (Who else? My adopted mommy. The mother of the weak and the dispossessed. You get my drift, I'll leave it here.)

HE: "Do you want me to take the poor darling home with me, so he's not all alone?"

The Damsel smiles inanely, moved by this heartfelt kindness. Her eyes shine. She gives him a grateful kiss. She knows the kind of burden an animal can be in a house. Especially an animal with long white hairs and extreme views on the love that endures all things and so on and so forth.

SHE: "You think?" (Imagine this "You think?" served up with a disgusting dose of coquettishness, which annoyed me no end. As if watching them salivate all over each other wasn't enough, I was now about to be turned into their third wheel?)

HE: "It's all settled then. We'll take him with us when I drive you to the airport and then I'll take him home." (He had the whole thing already planned, the sly bugger!)

SHE: "But it means carrying his litter and his food over and then carrying them back here . . . " (Why, the guy wouldn't have minded carrying the ocean with all its fish, if it served his purposes.)

He: "There's a pet shop around the corner. I won't be doing any carrying, hardly." (Damsel, whenever you see an excess of willingness, be suspicious. Do I have to teach you everything?)

SHE: "Well, since you insist, you can have him, what can I say?" (You can tell him to leave me in my peace and quiet.)

In actual fact, she didn't say anything at all to him. She kissed him. And then she picked up the last of her stuff, she put me inside the hateful carry basket (which ten times out of ten is used for no good purpose) and they offloaded me in the backseat of the car. I was feeling so let down by her attitude that I didn't even bother whining. After the tearstained farewell at the airport, Beefcake led me silently to his house. As soon as we arrived, he opened the door for me to get out but I stayed put, as good as dead. No, I am not stubborn or mean. But I can't stand human hypocrisy. I need for the masks to come off. And if there is something I've learned in my seven lives, my dears, it's that there is no better way to check someone's feelings than getting them irritated. (Meow No. 3467: Do any old blooper. The person in love will see it as a charming eccentricity and admire it. The person who loves you will be upset but will patiently try to understand your motives. And the one who couldn't care less is going to be livid.)

Beefcake was livid. After ordering me five times to "Get out!" he went back to his business saying, "You can sit there until kingdom come for all I care." He didn't go out to get me litter and he didn't get my any food. So, pal, is that how it's going to be? I thought. I'll show you! While he was busy at his computer, I quietly came out of the basket and left a huge turd on the hall rug. As you see, I was restrained. I could just as easily have decorated the Persian rug in the living room. Six hours later, he finally remembered my existence.

"Oh gee, Zach! I forgot to get you some food. What are you going to have now? Do you like eggplant salad?" (He hasn't yet seen the turd.)

I remain expressionless.

"No, huh? What shall I give you, then?" (He still hasn't seen the turd.)

I remain expressionless.

"You jerk, what have you done here? *I'm going to kill, you filthy thing!*" (He just saw the turd.)

I am still expressionless, only under the couch, just to be on the safe side.

Just about then the phone rang. It was the Damsel from Berlin. As soon as I heard him say her name, delighted, I ran toward him with my ears all pricked. At last, I thought, she had remembered me. She is calling to ask how her beloved Zach is coming along in his enforced house-sharing with this dude. Well, you can't imagine how very wrong I was, my dears. The unconscionable woman was calling to find out how her beloved Beefcake was coming along in his enforced house-sharing with me! As far as I could tell, she was even consoling him over my shitting on his carpet. I started meowing furiously. Tell her that you didn't get me any cat litter, you coward, I was screaming in felinese. Only, of course, there was no cat-to-human translation available on the premises.

I won't go into any more detail. I'll just say that, for a week, we lived like cat and dog, literally. When she finally got back from her stupid trip, she saw I was one kilo thinner but even that didn't rattle her.

"What happened? Why is he like this? Didn't little Zach eat?" (Madam can spare me the endearments. I have curtailed diplomatic relations with your good self.)

"How could he? He was missing you terribly . . . " he said. (Referring to himself again, of course.)

THE FELINE-NESS OF STRANGERS

No, don't hasten to come to any conclusions, my dears. I am NOT the jealous type. I am merely just. Instead of abstract arguments, let me present you the case of Mr. Tall. Now, here was a man dear to my heart! First of all, from the moment he set foot in the house, he showed me the respect that was mine by right. Because there is everywhere an invisible book of years, no two ways about it: I was with her for twelve whole years before he turned up. I knew both her good and (especially) her bad side, whereas he didn't know his head from his ass where she was concerned. All of this was taken into consideration. Let it be noted that: a) he had a dog at his house; and, b) he was allergic to my hairs. (The crowning glory of my Perfect Whiteness, that which distinguished me but also led to my downfall. The Damsel, as I have oft repeated, was sickened by the sight of them trailing like a plague on every fabric surface in the house. She never did get used to them. For fifteen whole years she called me "Mr. Molt." Her mother was loath to even sit in the living room. Many visitors, good friends though they were, came up in boils as soon as they came in contact with them due to allergy; as a result, the Damsel took to locking me out on the balcony for the duration of their visits. Have you any ideas how many parties I missed out on because of my hair? How many bucketfuls of petting? By the ocean shrimp, I had even contemplated going to the barber's and getting it shorn off, like Bruce Willis.

But Mr. Tall immediately loved the totality of me, hairs and all. Even more that, he became my personal advocate. When he would settle with the Damsel on the couch, not only did he not send me away, but persuaded her to let me snuggle in between them, be part of their company, cozily covered in a white fleece blanket with colored circles which I adored. He had slyly suggested it to me one day, as my hiding place: "Under here, Zach, this is where you should burrow; it's all white, like you, and nobody will be any the wiser." Whereas I would receive a pet every six months from the Damsel, I was getting an endless stream from him. He had even come up with a way for tricking the old allergy: He would pull his sleeves right down over his hands and use them as gloves, so he could pet me without coming out in a rash. (I know, I know, intimate contact is a worrisome and dangerous thing but if you set your mind to it, there are means and ways—isn't that right, Mr. Tall?)

The thing, though, I'll never forget, and for which I will forever be raining kisses on him from seventh heaven, is that for three years, he tried to get me inside the bedroom, in the face of strong opposition. At the beginning, he just opened the door for me to come in. The Damsel threw me out on the spot, before I had even a chance to see the color of the bedcovers. Once he realized that his mission was far from simple, he adopted a more orchestrated approach: a) the method of persuasion ("Come on, baby, look what a sweet thing he is, why can't we let him have a little corner somewhere?"); b) beseeching ("Come on, do it for me, I can't stand that imploring look in his eyes. No, it's no trick, he's going through some real heartache."); c) threats ("I swear I am going to report you to the RSPCA for cat abuse, I'm telling you!")

I had a lot of my hopes riding on Mr. Tall—maybe too many. I was hoping, for instance, that he might stave off her obsession with every so often grabbing a suitcase and disappearing for weeks on end. He himself was a couch potato, one of us. He wouldn't even go out to get cigarettes without his car. All this love, I kept thinking, has got to have an effect. Their first Christmas together she wouldn't, couldn't, leave him and disappear off to Alaska somewhere, I was thinking. Alright, she didn't go to Alaska, she went to the other end of the world, to a place called Fin Du Mundo, the World's End. Directly beneath lay the freezing Antarctic. He was freezing in Greece, waiting for her.

He didn't stop her from leaving for exotic locales, but I couldn't blame him for that—like I couldn't blame him for failing to curb the worst part of himself. In any event, we each sum up the records for our own private benefit. Nobody knows as well as we do just where we screwed up. And I'll always have a smile saved up for him on account of the following incident:

They'd slept in quite late on that occasion. (Nothing unusual about that. From the moment they met, those two never managed to go to sleep before six. They talked. Daylight came, the birds started singing in the garden next door and then, exhausted, they would decide to take a nap. What the hell they talked about during all those long hours, I have no idea. It goes without saying that I was glued to their door, eavesdropping, but unfortunately, I could only make out what was being said when there was a fight on. All the good bits slipped away and got lost. Nonsense. There's no way it got lost. Nothing gets lost. It's hiding somewhere, waiting. (Investment idea: If one day I find out where all the lost kisses and caresses are hiding, my dears, I will turn that place into the new Dubai of the heart. All the scorched hearts worldwide will come there to have healing love baths. I'll be a millionaire.)

The Damsel was the first to wake up at about noon. She left the room to make coffee, thinking Mr. Tall was still fast asleep. Appearances, however, can be deceptive and he was just playing possum for my sake. As soon as she was out of range, he

got up, quietly opened the door for me and let me sneak under the warm eiderdown in his arms. For about three minutes, I experienced heaven. The only thing missing was the mountains of fried sea bass. But no miracle lasts more than three days— or three minutes, as in the present case. The Damsel arrived with the coffees and she caught us at it, blissfully laid-back and content. Without a moment's hesitation she swooped down to grab me by the scruff of the neck but was stopped short by Mr. Tall. "Wait, just wait a moment before you throw him out." Immediately after that, he slunk back under the covers, so that no part of him was visible, his face included. "Now, do what you like," he mumbled from his hiding place. The Damsel unceremoniously dumped me in the hall, then went back and uncovered him. "What was that about? Why did you hide under there?" she asked him with genuine surprise. "I don't want him to associate me with his exile. I wanted him to see that I didn't agree," he said and smiled apologetically. (He didn't know it at the time but in the future, that one phrase would be his salvation from the most relentless enemy: forgetfulness, mine and hers.)

In general, I owe a great deal to the kindness of strangers— at least as much as Blanche Dubois. Her sister Smaroula and her best friend, Fillip, for instance, were always stroking me, from the moment they set foot in the house to when they left. The conversed and they stroked. They ate and they stroked. They idled and they stroked. Did she have to go live in Volos and he in London?

But my greatest love, the protector of all the weak and the dispossessed, human, canine and feline, was Christina, her other sister, who became my sister. In all the years I lived on this earth, the afternoons when Christina would come over for coffee were my birthday parties, my delight, my consolation. If it wasn't for her, I wouldn't have lasted through my endless days of solitude when the Damsel was clambering up and down mountain paths all over the globe. She didn't just nip in to feed me and then go. She came over, made coffee and kept me proper company. We even had our own ritual. As soon as she sat down, I immediately went up to her to see what she was wearing. If she was in jeans, I would jump straight up in her lap. If she had a dress on, I was more careful. First I reached with my paw, ascertained the robustness of the material, and then I adjusted my leap accordingly. But if she was wearing stockings, I never went up until she picked me up herself. The two sisters laughed themselves silly, watching my calculations. "Look at the trickster, figuring out what you're wearing to decide on his course," the Damsel would say. I was no trickster, madam. A gentleman is what I was. And, as is well-known, a gentleman never places a lady in an awkward position. All the more so if he has such a soft spot for her.

You mustn't think that I was happy to make the acquaintance of everyone who petted me, insofar as I met all sorts of people in the Damsel's living room. I am talking from the point of view of variety rather than numbers, because that woman may have appeared sociable and all the rest of it but, if you ask me, deep down she was very solitary. She could sit for days on end at her desk, in bed or on the carpet like a yogi, weaving (and unweaving) a story line in her head. She neither met with nor spoke to anyone. Me, well, you know me: despite the difficulty I have pretending to be a ghost, I was capable of a modicum of respect. In truth, I, too, am quite private, all my social graces notwithstanding. And if I'm telling this story, my dears, it's because I would very much like to advise some of you to keep a few things yourselves; not everything needs to be made public. Your quarrels, for example, can very well stay at home, can't they ? Do take pity on the rest of us and don't take them out to air and exercise them.

I will explain at once. I am no gossip, but I will never forget the evening when the Damsel and Ziggy had over for dinner a friendly couple, the kind whose conversation is made up of comments like, "The novel is dead, alongside individual responsibility and the social contract." The foodstuffs were ready, the tables were set—as I've had the opportunity to mention, the Damsel was an expert at throwing dinner parties. "A proper house needs cooking smells and the lights on" was her motto (alternating, of course, with "Leave me well alone, I don't give a hoot.") The doorbell rang at around nine. The Damsel ran to answer, all smiles. The evening was shaping up to be a very promising one. The guest was famous for his story-telling verve and his wife for her verve in general. Unfortunately, however, the verve turned to nerves. Two tight-lipped people appeared at the door who barely nodded "good evening" and then proceeded to sit at opposite ends of the couch, far from each other. One was facing toward the library in the hall and the other toward the table in the dining room. The Damsel and Ziggy, on the other hand, were facing each other, increasingly anxious. In vain they tried to get a word out of their visitors all through the evening. The select guests just sat there with their long faces, nervously jiggling their arms and legs and braying monosyllables at the questions of their hosts, who were getting more discomfited with every passing minute. At one point, the storyteller-who-wasn't picked me up and started stroking me nervously, evidently wanting to do something more constructive than jiggling his leg. Within five minutes I had run out of patience and good manners, too, and I escaped after scratching his right hand. "Strange, Zach never scratches," said the Damsel, relieved there was at last something to say. "Strange, the guest always talks," Ziggy whispered in her ear when they nipped into the kitchen to get some clear alcohol. I rubbed against his leg. You say it like it is, I meowed, gratified as always when someone in the house understood the spirit of justice that moved me.

If I had to name the greatest cult figure out of all the cat-loving crowd that paraded through that house, it would be a Dutch-Scotsman, fabulously gifted as a writer and one hundred percent mad. As soon as the guy clapped eyes on me, he asked the Damsel if I had an active sexual life. The Damsel stammered something about living on the fifth floor etc. and offered him a cup of tea (he didn't drink alcohol). Then, she closed the curtains (he couldn't bear the sun) and, after that, she heard him, openmouthed, advise her to buy me cat porn. He himself, living with his equally mad wife on some Scottish mountainside, had two cats, whom he regularly provided with cat porn. Looking into my eyes, he assured us that his cats were as happy as can be. For better or worse, I slunk off and hid under the washing machine. Call me a prude, but that isn't my definition of happiness.

THE MAN WHO SQUEEZED ORANGES

I n a few words, my dears, I lived long and saw many sights and many folks. I saw people who'd never grown up and others whose soul had fled from them at some point, leaving the body an empty husk. I saw people remain empty from the time they were born, like balloons—material designed exclusively for parties. I observed in terror as some folks were gradually displaced by another, stronger soul and henceforth remained homeless and invisible. I saw people as thick-skinned as pigs and others whose transparent skin barely contained the wound which was them. I have seen all of that without moving an inch from this deep red couch. There was only one whom I hadn't managed to see all those years: her dad, the mythical "Father" as the three sisters mock-lovingly called him.

I confess that with the years, my curiosity had reached quite a peak. As I pointed out previously, I am no gossip; it was just that the Father had become a kind of urban legend in the house. He was the invisible but indubitable protagonist in dozens of stories that caused paroxysms of laughter in friends and acquaintances. My favorite story was the one where the Father (who, I gathered, had taken on himself the role of safe-guarding, which is to say, monitoring, which is to say, policing the good health of his girls) secretly followed the ten–year-old Damsel to school to discover himself if she bought, on her own initiative, sweets, candies or takeaway treats of any description, which might in the future irrevocably undermine her sound health. The Damsel, healthy through no choice of her own, despite her generally scandalous good luck was on this occasion singularly unlucky. The Father put his detective plan in action on the one and only day when the young Damsel succumbed to the temptation of buying a bright red, delectable sugar apple from a vendor outside her school. At the very moment the poor lass reached to take a delicious bite into the forbidden fruit, she was stopped short by the Father's unexpected, drawn-out cry:

"You murderer of young children, do you know what carcinogenic coloring is in that rubbish you just sold my child?"

It doesn't take much to imagine the speed with which the "murderer" packed up and went off in search of new turf. He night as well have been dealing crack.

Apart from the endless stories, I also listened in to the phone calls the Father made to the now adult Damsel, living in Athens, all of which started with the same question: "How many oranges did you squeeze today?" Because, while some people believe in God, others in Buddha, others in the benevolent intervention of aliens, the Father believed in vitamin C: A large glass of fresh orange juice decimated, among other things, viruses, sexually transmitted diseases, cancer, constipation and depression. I had good reason to suspect that if the orange juice was absolutely fresh, it might also guarantee you perfect happiness!

His proverbial devotion to vitamin C (and his utter indifference to career, money and the rest of it) had even caused a legendary quarrel between daughter and father when the Damsel became a doctor of History after a great deal of toil, bibliographies, hardship, sleepless nights, self-doubting and footnotes. After she passed the orals without getting a heart attack, it was him she called first with the good news. There ensued the following exchange:

FATHER: "Hello, my child, how are things?" (In a voice

filled with anxiety because he always anticipated you were calling to announce some irredeemable health problem.)

The Damsel: "Fine, dad! I'm calling to say I passed with
honors. I am now a doctor!" (In a voice which, to be truthful,
was unabashedly triumphant.)

FATHER: "Well done, my child, well done." (In a rather
lukewarm tone.) "Did you squeeze yourself some oranges?"
(In a tone of voice avid with interest.)

The Damsel: "%&?$#@ GRRRRRRRRR @%&#!!!!!!"
(Unprintable comment!)

This, assuredly, was the Father's trademark: the unconditional love with which he had been dousing his daughters since
birth. They didn't need to be talented or widely acknowledged
or persuasive or clever or rich for him to love them. It was
enough that they were healthy and happy, a combination
which, as is well-known, no doctoral dissertation can provide.
Fresh orange juice does.

You might wonder how come, in all the years I was around,
I never did happen to see the Father? Where was I when he
came to Athens? Why, here is the crux, my dears. The Father
staunchly refused to set foot in the capital. This rule was subject to exception on only two occasions. The first was the christening of his grandson—I unfortunately missed the party as I
hadn't yet been born. Ever since then, no matter if there was a
marriage, a christening or a funeral, the Father had pulled back
and adamantly refused to visit the human rubbish dump called
Athens. He was, you see, a steadfastly monogamous lover of
Volos, his native city. "Listen, folks, I live by the sea and near
a mountain. I get on my bike and I am king of the world. Why
would I want to leave here?" he murmured in consternation
every time he suspected anyone of intending to pressure him
into visiting the smog capital.

So I had completely given up on ever seeing him, when the
miracle happened! Christina decided to marry and her Father,

though no fan of the institution of marriage, decided, nevertheless, to be present at the wedding. Naturally, he refused to stay longer than twenty-four hours. (That would have been a third miracle, but one mustn't be greedy.)

The Damsel was overjoyed and determined to make the best of this unique, historic conjunction. She outdid herself and prepared all her best dishes. She laid out a festive table in all the colors of the rainbow and invited the entire crazy family over, to witness the rare appearance of the paterfamilias. When they did all gather round the table, finally, I understood how the legend had been born. Apart from being larger than life, the Father made the funniest and most moving toast to the newlyweds. While his words were something to the effect of "What on earth were you thinking?" his eyes were wishing them the big wide sky with all its birds and the sea with all its fish. Next, he derided the unhealthy habits of everyone (to the Damsel, for instance, he pointed out she would do well to cancel her trip to Vietnam because the war was still going on down there, undeclared), he bade them not forget that vegetables save lives and all the while, he was casting smiling looks my way. He was very much an animal lover—in Volos he was feeding three stray cats, in addition to his own!

The three daughters had puffed up like balloons with pride and joy over having him with them, haranguing them for all the oranges they hadn't squeezed in a lifetime. I had settled in a corner unobserved amid the crowd and was carefully observing his expressions, all the things he wasn't putting in words, which is to say all the nicest bits. It was plain to see that he was taking mental photographs all the time of children and grandchildren eating and exchanging silly talk—he knew he wouldn't see them again all gathered around a table. That very knowledge made the night unforgettable. I always saw what humans couldn't see, you know that, my dears. That night I saw with perfect clarity above the table, the umbilical cords, the bonds connecting each to the rest, woven together inextricably over their heads, with the Father at the very middle. I was moved. So, that was why if you tripped one of them, they all fell. So, that is what we talk about, when we talk of love. Suddenly, I wanted my dad, too, but I had no idea who he might be or how to find him. My mom, on the other hand, I knew very well where she could be found, but I had no such desire, thanks very much. I leapt into the arms of the Damsel and snuck under her sweater. She was my mother. I was just keeping the news from her so she wouldn't get scared. I simply let my umbilical cord unfold outward and weave in with the rest of theirs.

THE VALLEY OF TEARS

The marriage took place and they lived happily ever after, and I, with my Damsel, lived even happier. Days passed that gathered into months, months passed that gathered into years, until one day in March when the phone rang in a very strange way. The Damsel ran to pick up. "Yes?" she said anxiously. "Mom?" I got worried. Her voice broke. Her face broke up. I hardly want to remember it, so I'll cut to the chase: Some foolish driver, the kind that speaks on her cell phone while driving, crossed into the oncoming traffic and hit him as he was taking his walk. The Father was rushed to intensive care and, as if by a fairy's magic wand, the whole family was immediately transported to his bedside, in the hospital in Volos. Under the general direction of Smaroula, who is a doctor there, the umbilical cords were woven again above his head, creating an invisible shield to keep death at bay. Left by myself, about three hundred kilometers away, I was trying to stretch my own, in case it managed to reach all the way there . . .

When the Damsel came back to our home, she was all wrapped in a black cloud. I was puzzled, I couldn't figure out her darkness. The Father managed to pull through, came out of intensive care and amazed everyone by how quickly he got out of bed, leaning on his walking frame. It didn't surprise me. He was a fanatic round-the-year swimmer, an all-weather cyclist, a man who never stood still. He knew how to live, as he himself put it. Well, after days and weeks of closely monitoring the Damsel and her conversations, I realized that this was precisely the problem that darkened our sun this spring of 1999. It was precisely because the Father knew how to live that he didn't want to live like this. He detested helplessness, being bedridden, pain, crutches, the smell of decay. And so he decided to die. He didn't do it at once, to give his girls time to prepare. He even told them: "My children, I was fooling time. It couldn't reach me because I was speeding away on my bike. Now, what needed to happen, has happened. I've been made to stand still and time has caught up with me. It's over." That is why on the night of October 8, after he fell asleep reading his newspaper in bed, he decided not to open his eyes again on this world. The country's financial and social crisis had been on its way for some time and there was no certainty whatsoever that vitamin C could provide an adequate defense.

Her mother woke her up at seven in the morning to tell her. (Now I understood why she had been sleeping with her cell phone by her pillow. She was waiting.) They only exchanged a couple of phrases. They were both shaking. The Damsel got up and started doing weird things. She spent about five minutes kissing me. Then she chose her best black clothes and started dressing very slowly. She was still shaking but for some strange reason, she was singing out of tune a song that went something like "*J'attendrais le jour et la nuit, j'attendrais toujours ton retour* . . ." I was meowing dolefully, rubbing against her legs—I didn't know what else to do. "That's the song he used to sing for us when we were little, my Zach," she said and kissed my ear. Then she went and threw the damned cell phone in the rubbish bin. Someone had to be punished for the bad news.

The world as we knew it was over.

GAME OVER

As I waited for her to come home after the funeral, I was wringing my head for ideas on how to bring her back to the present, as I knew with utter certainty she would come back a ten-year-old kid, all tearful and inconsolable. Indeed, when she came back, she was like an onion someone had started to peel. And as the peel fell away, the tears would come. You cannot imagine, my dears, the tricks I put to use to keep her afloat. I was wily, I did acrobatics, I pulled out all the stops. A doctor is what I turned into, to see her through. And when things became impossible, I would jump on the fruit bowl with the oranges and meow loudly. Have an orange juice, Damsel, you'll be yourself again.

Thus focused on her, I didn't see the signs. I was thirsty, my dears. All of a sudden, I would become very thirsty. My bowl kept emptying. The Damsel would absentmindedly fill it and I kept drinking on and on. I didn't have time to think about myself and she didn't suspect anything. And you know what someone is like who doesn't want to think of the worst. As impenetrable as a wall.

But a day came when I was forced to confront it, whether I wanted to or not. I had become heavy. And the thirst had become unbearable. So, that was it? Have you grown old, my boy? How did my days on earth pass so quickly? When was all my time used up? Impossible to conceive. April isn't the cruelest month, October proved worst, despite what my beloved T. S. Eliot says. (And, by and large, that poet knows what he's talking about, my dears, he's no idle talker. He's taken up all the truly great subjects: the loneliness of contemporary man, cats, the existential despair of postindustrial civilization et cetera.) The funny thing is that both she and I thought we had all the time in the world. Cats, see, aren't aware of the concept of time and humans ignore the facts that don't suit them. We were certain, as a result, that we had days and nights ahead, followed by more days and nights, all at our disposal to caress and bond with each other, to open up and close up again, to love and be willful with each other. We were possessed of this secret certainty that we would always be together, dancing our interminable waltz of war, with an inexhaustible fund of love always at our disposal. But no. Of course not. Everything is as illusory as a dream. All who loved us are as shooting stars that light us up momentarily, change us and are gone. Great haste makes great waste, is what I used to believe. Now, I didn't have that much time anymore.

That is how the great downhill course began. I was rotting on the inside, while on the outside my Perfect Whiteness remained resplendent. I was like the apple with the worm. A magic picture. I jumped two meters in the air, I teased and did backflips—I was acting the eternal youth though I was a fifteen-year-old senior citizen. I intentionally overturned my bowl of water so she wouldn't realize I was emptying it with alarming frequency. I was praying for the picture to hold up for as long as possible, the wrapping. She mustn't see that I, too, would be leaving her. A bit of time is what I needed, just a small reprieve. She wouldn't be able to take any more peeling back just at that moment. Besides, I didn't want her mercy. What I had always wanted was her love. Total and unconditional. Enough so that it would open a road for me to get inside her, finally. Give me a bit more time, I was praying to the unknown gods. I wanted to give my all, now that I could hear the frozen footsteps of the end approaching, to be more sugar-

like, more lovable, more smart and wily. Will I be able to make
her see me at last, as a character in a novel? How did Puss in
Boots manage it? The Cheshire Cat? Sylvester? Tom? What
did Fritz the Sly have that I don't? Why the hell hadn't I managed, in all the years, to make something of myself—a Greek
version of a Robin Hood for cats, which would fit in with my
altruistic personality?

But the signs were multiplying fast. My ignominious body
was betraying me. I started going to the toilet on the carpet.
Thankfully, instead of worrying, she scolded me. She thought
it yet one more of my whims. "You little bastard, do that again
and I swear I'm going to kill you," she yelled, throwing a slipper. Instead of ducking I went to her and looked her in the eye.
You don't need to trouble yourself, Damsel, I'm on my way out
anyway, I said. Only she couldn't hear me.

Until, finally, I admitted it. I had no more time. I wasn't
going to get her to love all of me nor would she let all of me get
in one of her books. That's alright, I said inwardly. I loved you,
Damsel, and that will be your punishment when I am no longer
around. It is now time for us to begin our parting waltz.

Prana? What prana?

When you ask for something, it comes, as you well know. So, to our home that night came Cassandra, an accomplished actor and, as it turned out, a veritable animal lover. The Damsel didn't know her very well, she had come over to discuss business. But fate, my dears, always does arrive in disguise, does it not? Cassandra sat on the couch, paid me the appropriate attention and, then, they starting talking about their professional plans. I didn't leave their side for a moment. I knew what they didn't, you see, so I waited. When they were done, the Damsel announced to Cassandra that she was going to be out of Athens for seventeen days. It was Christmas and the next day she was leaving for the Gran Sabana in Venezuela. The hateful backpack and the rest of the accessories were packed and safely stashed as always in the bedroom, to keep them safe from my spiteful scratching. She was so excited that she would be climbing on the mythical Indian tepui Roraima[2] that she spent half an hour talking about it to poor Cassandra, leaving her dazed.

In her turn, Cassandra told her that she was also going away, to Thailand, not for holidays or for an acting gig, but to do some training in prana healing! The Damsel looked at her askance. What on earth was that? Cassandra patiently explained that the aura, the energy field that surrounds all

[2] Translator's Note "Tepui" means "house of the gods" and refers to the tabletop mountains (or mesas) to be found in the Guiana Highlands of South America, especially in Venezuela.

creatures, bears the imprint of every problem of the soul and body and that healers can make a diagnosis and, often, effect a cure. The Damsel listened, impressed though unconvinced.

"Well, how exactly do you do the diagnosis?" she asked. "Can you do one with little Zach here so I can see it?"

I took a step forward, offering myself. Here is the moment you've been waiting for, my boy, I thought. Be strong now. Cassandra stroked me to calm me, spread her hands and started feeling my aura beginning at the head and moving to the tail. She was smiling at first and nodding encouragingly at the Damsel, who was biting her nails. Everything fine. Everything perfect. But when she reached my lower legs, she started frowning. She was a good woman, I could feel it in her hands.

"Please, you need to take him to the doctor, first thing tomorrow," she said to the Damsel.

The poor love was completely unprepared. Going into a mild shock, she sank back in the couch. In order not to let the bad omen in, she started on a barrage of questions:

"The doctor? But why should I take him to the doctor? Can't you see he is fine? He eats and he drinks and he frolics like always. He's as healthy as can be. Besides, tomorrow I'm leaving for Venezuela, first thing in the morning. I don't have the time. But why take him, anyway? Can't you see he's bursting with health?"

Fine, Damsel, we get it. You are only human. You believe that if you declare me healthy a dozen times in a row, then that's what I'll be.

Seeing her response, Cassandra realized she had no other option. She needed to be direct with her.

"I have no choice but to be frank with you; Zach has a serious problem with his kidneys. The left one is no longer working, and the right is only partly functional."

I shall never forget the stages of the Damsel's mental reaction when she heard the bad news. I saw on her face surprise, doubt, sadness and denial succeed one another like masks. Naturally, denial carried the day.

"Prana? What prana?" she told me next morning as she was zipping up her pack and saying goodbye. "You are just fine, my Zach!"

GOODBYE AND FARE THEE WELL

Seventeen horrid days went by. The house was empty
without the Damsel and I, too, was being emptied out of
life. I became unrecognizable. What a joke to see it so
suddenly: She had been keeping me together. That's how it
always happens. We live holding on to the love of the others.
As soon as they leave us, we fall.

On the night of her return I heard, as always, the car stop-
ping in front of the building and the unloading of her stuff. I
heard her come in the front door downstairs, call the elevator
and come up the five floors. But I didn't have the strength to
go meet her meowing happily like I had done all these years.
The ritual of her return had always been the same. I would
meow myself hoarse and she would hear me from the elevator
and laugh. "Stop yelling, fatso, I'm coming", she'd say as she
unlocked the door. As soon as she came in, she would glance
at me and then scan the house. She had a sharp eye, alright,
that took everything in. The flowers I had chewed, the sand I
had trailed into the living room, one revengeful little turd on
the carpet, a book dragged under the table, a snowstorm of
hairs on all the living room pillows. "You wrecked the place
again, fatso, didn't you?" she grumbled instead of hugging me.
She wanted to, I could tell, but she always played high and
mighty and hard to get. She used my hair to avoid admitting,
at long last, that she adored me, that she missed me, that she
was overjoyed I always anticipated her return so eagerly. I, of
course, kept it up undeterred. I clung to her like her shadow,

meowing, "Here I am, silly, give me a hug, you've left me all these days by myself." Sometimes, in order for her to see me, I leapt up onto the kitchen table and called to her from there. That always made her break up: "Look at you, little pest, finding just the spot to watch me all the better," she'd say. And then, finally, she'd plant a kiss on my ear. My favorite!

"Jaaacques! My little Jaaacques!" I heard her voice calling as she unlocked the apartment door. "Where are you, fatso? You're not being willful, now, are you?" (Oh, Damsel, you really don't want to believe it, do you? When was I ever willful?) She burst in and for the first time in her life, she dropped the mountaineering gear and started searching for me in one room after the other. I tried to meow but her voice covered mine. Finally, mad with anxiety, she turned on the kitchen light and saw me. I'll only say this, my dears: It would have been much better if I had ascended to the heavens. I wish she had never seen me in the state I was in. I was a skeleton, perched on the sink, my fur filthy (not my fault! I could no longer give myself a tongue bath) my head wet from the water dripping on it (I was so thirsty, it was imperative to be next to water—me, who loathed it so much!). A mixture of blood and saliva dripping from my mouth. What can I say . . . It was a blessing there was no mirror anywhere near. As self-conscious about my appearance as I was, I would have committed suicide had I suddenly caught a glimpse of myself.

The Damsel grabbed me in her arms, cleaned me up and dried me, while crying inconsolably. She had understood. All the days she lived away from me, all the mornings she didn't let me under her bedcovers, all the caresses she never gave me, rose up and started demanding justification. Don't cry, Damsel, I wanted to say. Let bygones be bygones. I want to remember you smiling, O.K.?

That night, we slept together. As soon as it was morning, she wrapped me in my favorite white blanket and took me to the neighborhood vet. He was a quack—she was the one who came up with the diagnosis in his place. She had already searched on the Internet and found that malfunctioning kidneys affect the teeth. Cassandra had been right. That's why my gums were bleeding. That's why I desperately wanted water. That's why I was in the process of collapsing.

The doctor recommended a special dietary regime of croquettes for cats with failing kidneys plus some prescription medicines. The Damsel left me in my nest and ran out to get them. I instantly rejected them, naturally. Come now, Damsel, I told her, swishing my tail. I only have a few days left, spare me this tasteless stuff and these pills and get me some ocean shrimp. It's my farewell party we're talking about—let's live it up like there's no tomorrow!

It has been mentioned before: When it came to throwing a party, she was second to none! She and I reached an instant, and perfect, understanding. The pills and the rest went into the rubbish bin and I was feasting again on my beloved shrimp. For a week, I seemed to be O.K. again. I don't know how come—maybe her feverish wish to make me well, what with all the energy she poured into me, revived me. It was the happiest week of my life. The Damsel rarely went out so she wouldn't leave me on my own. Finally, we were having our honeymoon. We were literally glued to each other. She let me sneak slowly under her cardigan and reach up to her neck, she kissed my ears (first the left, then the right, my favorite), we slept together, we were touching constantly—the miracle had come to pass: She had at long last become a cat and I had become human! I was so immensely pleased that I would gladly exchange ten years of normal living for another week like this one. I, the sleepyhead, hardly slept anymore: My hours were precious. You can sleep when you're dead, my boy, I told myself as I watched her sleeping next to me, lawfully at last! When she woke up, I tried to make her look me in the eye to greet her, to say to her that I was O.K. with never managing to be turned into a book, it was more than enough that I was her beloved. (You don't know this, my dears, but that is how we get into your mind and talk to you without words, by looking at you straight in the eye.) I was impossible. She couldn't bear it. My strange eyes, one lettuce-green, one sea-blue, had always been her weakness. Impossible to watch them fade away. So, to avoid them, she hugged me to her.

Then the countdown began. Day by day I was getting thinner, whittled away. After a while, I could no longer move. I stayed put, inside a kind of nest she'd made for me, with my head literally hanging inside a large bowl of water. We both knew it—my time had come. Still, it was hard for her. Mighty hard. For years, I'd heard her speeches in favor of euthanasia, how she would gladly help any loved one to make an exit, help them maintain some dignity in their last hour. But theory is one thing and practice is quite another. If only you knew what compassion I felt for her in those hours she spent hovering above me and stroking me with shaky hands. She knew she had to do something, she couldn't allow my humiliation to go on and on. "Zach," she would whisper in my ear, "my fatso, what shall I do? I can't make you well, and I can't help you make your exit. And in three days I have to go to the literary festival in Berlin; how am I ever going to leave you here to find your way out by yourself?" I, who always ran to her when she called, hated to let her down, even now. I did my best and managed to move my tail a little. I hear you, I was saying to her, not to worry, everything is going to be alright.

Which means that my guardian angel (and hers) Christina would take it on herself to free me from this derelict body in which I've been trapped. That same afternoon Christina turned up and made the suggestion. She knew that you had taken me twice to the doctor and that both times you came back in tears, with nothing to show for it. "I will look after lit-

tle Zach," she said. "While you are in Berlin. I won't tell you
when it's going to happen. But when you get back, everything
will have been taken care of." I gave everything I had to meow
("Hurrah!") but nothing came out.

In the night, I dreamt we were living our love backwards.
From the end back to the beginning. Leaving behind the tears
of the end, we moved day by day backwards, full of hope for
the excitement of the first meeting. The dream finished when I
became again a white fluffy ball who, after meeting you, ran off
and disappeared forever behind Madam Sweetie's bushes . . .

Hello and goodbye, Damsel.

RISEN FROM THE DEAD

Before leaving for the airport, she had left on the kitchen table the fleecy white blanket with the colored circles. On it she had pinned a note: *Wrap him up in this to keep him warm. It's his favorite.*

Christina helped me cross the wide river in two wraps: my blanket and her love. I won't say more.

The point is that when the injection was given, I felt like a door had been thrown open. I was now free, a perfectly white, fuzzy light on a journey, here, everywhere and nowhere, all at the same time. Happy again. But what about her? I needed to make sure she was alright before I left for good. If I met the Father over there in the depths of the hereafter, swimming in a lake of orange juice, he would crucify me for abandoning her on some airport escalator. So I dived in a northern direction and with a whooshing sound I found myself in Berlin. I flew over the Ku'damm, flew over Fazantstraat, then over the kitchen of my namesake, Zach H. There they were, sitting at the large kitchen table, having coffee and chocolates. The Damsel was smoking with one hand and wiping tears with the other. I was the subject of their conversation. My namesake was trying to come up with some words of comfort. Wise though he was, he couldn't find any. Now that I mention it, I always knew it wouldn't be easy for me to be forgotten. I really was sweet!

"I can't believe that when I walk in the door he won't be there. How is it possible that I'm never going to see him again? Not ever?"

Zach H. then took her hand and said something unexpected:

"Don't cry, you will see him before you all the time, when you least expect it."

She raised her eyes, full of childlike expectation.

"Really?" she said. "Where?"

"Look behind you," Zach quietly said and pointed to the tableau with all his photographs up on the kitchen wall.

The Damsel turned slowly and saw me looking at her straight in the eye from my picture. It had been there for years. She herself had made a gift of it to him (*from Zach to Zach*) but she had forgotten. Now the old photograph was shining, animated, because I had sneaked into it a mere second before. Which is why, the exact moment she looked at it, her eyes locked with mine. AT LAST! AT LONG LAST! Damsel, look at me, I am right here! Will you listen to me already?

The Damsel smiled, came close, stroked me, sat back down in her chair and, smiling even more broadly, she said:

"Zach, darling, I just got a crazy idea: I'm going to write little Zach' memoirs!"

YES!YES!YES!YES!YES!YES!YES! My dears, I made it!

With another whooshing sound I ascended to heaven after casting one last look at her. She had dried her tears and was excitedly explaining her plan to him. Mission accomplished, then, do you read me, my dear Cheshire Cat? I, too, did your trick: I have departed, indeed I have, but I left my smile behind. Forever.

ABOUT THE AUTHOR

Lena Divani was born in Volos, Greece. She is the author of novels, short stories, and plays. This is her first novel to appear in English.